Charlie's Encore

J. RONALD M. YORK

ACKNOWLEDGEMENTS

This book would have not been possible without
the help and guidance from
Mary Helen Clarke, Ralph Henley, Allan Musto, Rebecca
Pierce, Carol Poston, Lynette Sesler, and Vicki Shipley

Cover illustration Red Hot Grand!
Artist – Ron York

PROLOGUE

Is it possible for a fault line to occur in the human heart? A break or split that might not be obvious to others? I believe that happened to me at the close of 2019. Then, a few short months into the year 2020, an event so traumatic caused a shift that allowed my already fractured heart to shatter.

My name is Ricky Hunt, and for forty-plus years, I have worked in the interior design field in Hillmont. It was always my first choice – my first love. However, I retired a few years back, sold my home and furnishings, moved into a high-rise condominium, and wrote a book – *Nathaniel & the Midnight Movers*. It was marketed as a novel and, yet, if I'm being truthful, it was actually a memoir – a tell-all or confessional. Please, allow me to explain.

I've been lucky to have two groups of friends whom I could call family. In my youth, they consisted of college roommates, lovers, and ex-lovers. Close friends bound together by secrets and lies. You see, we *were* a gang of thieves. And yes, I was Nathaniel, and my friends were the Midnight Movers. For several years we robbed furnished models, houses, condos, and more. We took unnecessary risks and yet, miraculously avoided arrests. I've stayed in contact with only two of the remaining five members – Bill, my ex from forty years ago, and Greg, my college roommate, who introduced me to Bill.

And, there was Dean – my beautiful redheaded freckled-face former classmate, roommate and partner in crime who moved in and out of my life. Addictions and bad choices had taken their toll on Dean until his heart gave out at the age of forty-two. It was then that I learned he had turned his life around, remarried, and fathered a child.

My second family materialized a couple of years ago when Jeff, a longtime friend and former design client, introduced me to James Norris. Jim had written a book about a peeping Tom who was blackmailing a therapist. Jim's book, *Peeper*, was presented as a novel. And, like my book, it was more truth than fiction. When I first met Jim, he was in a relationship with Matt, who was the therapist from his book. Jim had unexpectedly become entangled in Matt's drama involving Matt's ex-wife and her brother. The events that transpired in those few short months brought in Diana, an agent with the State Bureau of Investigation.

As Jim's "novel" gained notoriety, an episode where the peeping Tom rescued a young boy from a sexual predator was revealed to be true. Dylan, the young boy – now a young man – had come forward after he read Jim's book.

Jeff was a columnist for the Arts & Entertainment section of the local newspaper. His review of Jim's book *Peeper* is what triggered Dylan, a waiter at Jeff's favorite restaurant, to read it – and realize his personal connection.

Jim, Matt, Diana, Jeff, Dylan, and yours truly formed a bond. Roberta Ann, the queen of estate sales, joined us as Jim and I had done business with her.

How did 2020 break my heart, you ask? As I said, it began in 2019, when we learned Matt's façade of a decent, understanding therapist was a lie. He, along with his ex-wife Julie, and her brother Chris, who as it turned out was Matt's lover, are currently serving time in prison for their actions.

And then, there was the heartbreaking loss of our dear, much-loved friend Jeff when cancer took him from us in December.

Jim dealt with the accusations as the secrets in his book came to light. Fortunately, my "novel" had flown under the radar. However, Jim was harassed when the drama surrounding him caught the media's attention. His agent seized the momentum, and landed Jim a national magazine review. A guest spot on *The Tonight Show* never happened because in the spring of 2020, Jim was brutally murdered. Without Jeff and Jim, my second family had lost the ties that bound us together.

Meanwhile, our country had descended into chaos and became divided by a contentious presidential election that resulted in four hellacious years. Friends and family members parted ways over lies and propaganda. I walked a thin line between wanting to be informed and yet becoming enraged or even more depressed whenever I watched the news.

Then, as if it couldn't get any worse, the pandemic hit. COVID-19 was unlike anything we had ever seen. And as a gay man, I had lived through and lost way too many friends to AIDS in the 1980s and 1990s. Our leaders were scrambling to figure things out, but handled things poorly. Misinformation spread like wildfire. Sides were chosen and opinions formed as people dug in their heels and refused to listen to facts. As the virus spread throughout the world, our new reality felt like a science-fiction movie.

People hunkered down – another excuse that made it easy for our "family" to disband. Businesses closed, and those that survived were forced to reinvent the way they operated. It became easy to distance yourself from friends, co-workers and loved ones – to step back from relationships with those who looked at the world in a radically different way or were in denial. Masks, sometimes mandated, were worn to protect not only yourself but others as well. Vaccines became available, and yet so many resisted until it was too late.

As I step cautiously into the new year, I'm reminded of a quote credited to the late Dorothy Parker whenever her phone or doorbell would ring: "What fresh hell is this?"

CHAPTER

"Ricky?" Gayle asked, then snapped her fingers. "Ricky? Are you with us?"

"What?" I replied after Mike nudged my side.

A group of us were sitting in Charlie's, the oldest gay/ lesbian bar in Bellwood. I was visiting my friend – boyfriend, lover, whatever – Mike for the weekend. We had been together for three, no, four years after reconnecting decades later from our first introduction when we were part of the wedding party for Dean and Karen.

"I asked if you were still with us," Gayle replied. "It felt like you had drifted into your own little world."

"Sorry," I apologized. "I know I don't share the history that you do with this bar, but I couldn't help but look around and remember some of the good times over the years."

"Good and bad," added Mike.

"True," I agreed. "The first time I entered that door, it was called Sugar's. His portrait, along with garish Christmas lights, hung over the bar."

"And then Charlie secretly bought it – something none of us knew until he died and left it to Peggy," added Val.

"Well, Mike and I knew," Bobby reminded us.

"But, Peggy has kept Charlie's memory alive," Val continued, "and now it's his portrait that hangs over the bar."

Charlie's was in the middle of a rundown row of businesses. It was a shotgun space with booths on the left side and the bar on the right. A small dance floor and jukebox remained in the back corner near the restrooms. Peggy had refurbished the space when she first inherited it and continued to slap a new coat of paint on the walls every few years. But still, it looked rough. Even with the lights dimmed, you could tell it was worn and tired. Not unlike us – seven "seniors" mostly in our sixties with Peggy, the oldest, rockin' her seventies.

"I don't mean to be rude, but..." I continued, "isn't the crowd rather sparse for a Friday night?"

"It is what it is," Peggy replied. "For years, we were the only game in town, but now, two other bars have opened, attracting the younger set and those who like to watch them."

"One is a dance bar," Char explained. "They play music so loud that you couldn't have a conversation if you tried. Does that make me sound old?"

"Yes, but it's true," added Val, receiving a glare. "Plus, everyone looks like they're about twelve years old."

Val still wore her hair short, although it was now gray, and her clothes were understated and tailored. Char's soft waves remained blonde with an expensive cut. Her outfit, more relaxed than what she used to wear to work, was feminine and stylish. The two of them had been together longer than any of our relationships, and they married a few years back.

"I went there once, and that was enough," Bobby revealed. "Young guys kept hitting on me, hoping I'd buy them a drink. I may be old enough to be a sugar daddy, but I'd prefer not to be."

"Speaking of which," Peggy began, "weren't you seeing someone a while back?"

"Yes, but he wasn't *that* young," Bobby explained. "We just didn't have much in common. And yes, he always expected me to pick up the check."

"How young was he?" I asked.

"Thirty-something," Bobby answered sheepishly.

"That's half your age," Mike exclaimed. To which Bobby raised his hand, then his middle finger.

Bobby was still attractive, with his hair more salt than pepper. The few extra pounds he carried kept his skin looking youthful. He and Mike had been a couple for years and eventually grew apart but have remained the closest of friends.

Mike, now *my* Mike, was still handsome in a distinguished way. Fit and trim with silver hair and an infectious smile. He had given up wearing contacts some time ago for stylish eyeglasses that projected a look much more serious than his upbeat personality.

"What about the other bar?" I asked, changing the subject.

"Leather," Peggy replied.

"There are that many queens in Bellwood who are into leather and can support a bar?" I asked.

"There are the serious leather freaks, the wannabes, and those who admire them," Bobby ticked off. "And before you ask, I also stopped in there once out of curiosity. They even have a back room, but I wasn't comfortable going in there."

"Were you wearing leather?" I asked.

"Or Naugahyde®?" Mike quickly added with a smirk before Bobby could answer.

"Well, I had on jeans, a leather belt, and leather shoes," Bobby replied. "Does that count?"

"And you think these two bars have affected your business?" I asked Peggy.

"The dance bar, for sure," she answered. "You remember back when you were a cute young thing wanting to get out there on the floor and shake it, right? I can't blame them. We've got this postage stamp of a dance floor with a jukebox. They've got a dance floor the size of a three-car garage and a DJ. I can't compete with that."

"And the leather bar?" Mike inquired.

"I see it as a novelty that might wear off," she explained. "Plus, from what I've heard might be going on in their back room, I won't be surprised if the law steps in one day. And, there goes their liquor license."

"Pity," Karen said sarcastically.

"We did have a good December," Peggy continued. "And a decent New Year's Eve crowd. But, here we are in mid-January, and it has died down again."

Peggy, Dean's oldest sister, was married until her husband walked out on her. She moved home to Bellwood to look after her parents, and met the infamous Charlie, who saw a need in her – a missing spark – and convinced her to help out at the bar. None of us could believe it when her gloom and doom personality was lifted. Peggy was the perfect fit and bonded with Charlie, proving to be his rock, his guardian angel to the end. Her red hair was now silver and her figure matronly. She looked like someone's sweet grandmother, but deep down, she could be a real ball-buster.

"So, what are you going to do about your competition?" I asked.

"Well, my niece has some ideas," Peggy shared.

"Niece? As in your evil sister Alice's daughter?" I asked in disbelief.

"That would be the one," our waitress inserted into the conversation as she set another glass of Chardonnay in front of Karen.

"You?" I asked. "Your mother is Alice? You are – wait a second – you're Margaret?"

"I prefer Maggie," she replied.

I had not noticed her until now, but I could see the family resemblance. Probably no more than 5′ 3″ tall, with a slender frame. Her hair was a combination of her parents – red from her maternal relatives mixed with brown from her father's side – a striking auburn color pulled back in a ponytail.

"I forgot to tell you about that," Mike said, turning to me. "Maggie's been working here for about six months."

"And it has been almost a year since I've been in Charlie's," I mumbled.

"I know. I didn't even learn that you were in town until after you left," Peggy said. "I was beginning to think you were mad at me – at all of us. Or that I had pissed you off."

"That's always a possibility," Val added.

"No, that wasn't it," I began. "With everything that happened, I just haven't been in the best of moods."

"I can confirm that," Mike said, then added, "Sorry."

"No, it's true. So much drama, so much loss. I couldn't come to terms with everything," I explained. "It's still hard to comprehend what happened in such a short period of time."

"Your friend who was murdered?" Maggie asked. "Brutally murdered? Peg told me about it."

"Yes, and another dear friend with a big heart who lost his battle with cancer."

"The one who was murdered was the peeping Tom perv, right?" asked Val. "I'm surprised it didn't happen sooner."

"Say that again, and I'm out of here," I snapped a little too sharply. "You don't know one thing about him. What a fucking insensitive thing to say."

"Ricky," Mike began.

"Don't defend her," I said to Mike.

"I'm sorry," Val began. "You're right. I shouldn't have said that."

"But, you still think it, don't you?" I asked. "Let me guess... you read his book, learned it was true, and formed an opinion of what you think he was like? Jim had made amends for his past."

"Plus, he saved that young boy– what's his name?" Char began.

"Dylan," Mike answered.

"Yes, Dylan. He stepped in and rescued him," Char stated.

"Yes, I know," Val barked. "I messed up. I'm sorry. I don't know what else I can say."

"One day, when you're up to it," Karen, the peacemaker, said sweetly, "please tell us about Jim. It's not fair for any of us to judge him without knowing the Jim you knew. And, God knows, we've all got some shit in our past."

Karen had married and divorced Dean. She always regretted how their marriage ended. Then, she remarried a cheating snake who was more than ready to burst out of his closet. It was an ugly situation, according to Mike. But she landed on her feet and partnered with Bobby to run a successful florist business. Karen looked closer to fifty-nine than sixty-nine. She was trim and coloring her hair lighter and softer than the dark brown I remembered from college.

"Thank you," I replied in a much calmer tone. Then, turning to Maggie: "Now, young lady, how did you end up at Charlie's?"

"First of all, remind me never to piss you off," she began with a smile. "If you think my mother was upset at Peggy for owning a gay bar, you can imagine what her response was finding out her only daughter was a lesbian?"

"I would have expected her to have hired an exorcist," I replied as everyone chuckled.

"If only," Maggie continued. "Basically, I'm dead to her."

"As your mother, my sister, is to me," Peggy added.

"So, I called my aunt Peg, and here I am," Maggie concluded.

"Tell them your ideas," Peggy encouraged, motioning for Maggie to pull up a chair at our makeshift booth with an added table and chairs.

"A piano bar and restaurant," Maggie announced.

"You're going to open a restaurant?" Karen asked Peggy.

"Not me," Peggy replied. "Maggie."

"What?" Bobby began.

"Look, I'm seventy-four. It's time for me to retire," Peggy informed us.

"But you can't retire," Val argued.

"You're younger than me, and you're retired. And so is Char. Although I can't imagine the Cadillac dealership surviving without the two of you."

"I have a friend who mentioned the service department isn't the same without Val in charge," Karen shared.

"And you and Bobby sold the florist," Peggy continued looking at Karen. "Taking it easy now, right?"

"I continue to help out with some of their bigger events," Bobby explained.

"And, I work a wedding here and there," Karen added.

"Because you want to – not because you have to work," Peggy stated. "And Mike, I know you're doing fewer design jobs by choice, for friends or really good clients."

"True," Mike admitted.

"Girl, I hear ya," I chimed in. "I'm retired and loving it. Although there are times that I wish I had something more to occupy my mind."

"Again, I'm the oldest in the group and still working six days a week," Peggy said. "I'd rather Maggie take over and let me help part-time if she needs me."

"Restaurant?" I repeated. "Any experience?"

"I worked in food service for nearly eighteen years," Maggie announced.

"Eighteen? Child, how old are you?" I asked.

"Forty-three."

"Older than Bobby's boyfriend," Mike said, laughing.

"And what about the piano bar idea?" Char asked.

"We can't compete with the dance bar, even if we wanted to," Maggie began. "There isn't enough space, and seriously, who wants that constant thump – thump – thump blasting night after night?"

"But the jukebox?" Val pleaded.

"The jukebox stays," Peggy assured her. "The piano bar would be Thursday through Sunday, as would the food service. At least to start."

"We'll still be closed on Mondays and stay pretty much the way we are now on Tuesday and Wednesday. Jukebox and drinks with limited, but much better quality, snacks," explained Maggie. "And the jukebox will be available between sets on the nights we have entertainment."

"A quiet, sophisticated place for cocktails and conversation," Karen summarized.

"And, maybe in time, we'll do a Sunday brunch with drag queen servers and performers," Peggy said. "It seems to be a popular idea in other cities."

"Back to the 'sophisticated place' Karen mentioned earlier," Mike began. "Don't take this the wrong way, but sophistication is not what comes to mind when I think of Charlie's. And you're not changing the name, are you?"

"No, it will stay Charlie's. His portrait will continue to hang over the bar, along with the years of photos of you guys behind plexiglass," Maggie explained.

"But, it *will* get a facelift," Peggy added. "You know, a second act – an encore."

"Charlie's Encore has a nice ring to it," Karen repeated.

"Or, Charlie's Second Act," added Val.

"Charlie's Piano Bar? Or, Cocktail Lounge?" inserted Gayle.

"What about Charlie's Toe-Tap Room?" Bobby asked, laughing.

"Charlie's Quarter-Note Lounge? Charlie's Eighty-Eight?" Char offered, then clarified. "You know, eighty-eight keys on a piano."

"All good ideas," Maggie admitted.

"As I was saying," Peggy announced, taking back control of the conversation. "I'd like the two of you to come up with an affordable design concept."

"The two of us?" I asked for Mike and myself.

"What else do you have to do?" Peggy inquired. "After all,

you're retired, and Mike's slowing down."

"And there you have it," Gayle said with a chuckle.

"Where's Connie tonight?" Karen asked Gayle. Connie and Gayle had been good customers back in the days when Karen worked at Suzy-Q's women's shop at the mall.

Gayle had been Dean's high school sweetheart and would often double-date with Mike and Connie. Gayle and Connie were childhood best friends. They reminded me of Veronica and Betty from the *Archie* comic books. Gayle kept her hair colored its original brunette, straight and shoulder-length. And Connie kept hers "natural" blonde. Mike had reconnected with them at Dean's memorial service.

"I told her I'd pick her up, but she said she had other plans," Gayle shared. "I asked her what they were, she hesitated, and then finally said to ask Mike. Care to explain?"

"Let's not get into this tonight," Mike replied. "We're having such a good time."

"Okay, now you've got to tell us what's up," Peggy demanded. "What did you do?"

"Why would you assume it's my fault?" Mike asked.

"This sounds worse than I thought," added Gayle.

"Spill," Val demanded.

"Guys, let it go, please," I pleaded for Mike's sake. I knew why Connie wasn't there.

"Nope," Gayle said. "Connie's part of this group. I want to know what happened."

"Politics," Mike said with resolve.

"You've got to be kidding," Char reacted. "Didn't we learn during those four years from hell to never discuss politics?"

"And, aren't we all on the same page?" Val asked.

"No, Connie's opinion is different from mine," Mike began. "I realized that early on and tried not to bring it up."

"How did we not know this?" Peggy asked. "Oh, wait, you're right, Char. We tried to never talk about politics. And then when we did, I guess Connie kept quiet."

"That means her stance is different than mine," stated Char.

"And mine," added Val.

"Same," Bobby said, with Karen adding, "me, too."

"I've made no secret as to where I stand," Peggy announced. "And Maggie feels the same."

"Gayle?" Bobby asked.

"Let's drop it," Gayle suggested.

"No way," Val retorted. "You wanted an explanation. You don't get to shut down the conversation if it's not going the way you want."

"Guys, seriously, maybe we should stop," I pleaded again, hoping to avoid hurt feelings.

"Okay, I didn't vote the same as you," Gayle said with attitude. "I felt we needed a change. While I wasn't sure about my choice, I had to believe he would be better than the alternative. Plus, he was saying things that I agreed with, making promises that I know didn't come true – but at the time, it felt right. Would I vote for him again? No. In fact, I didn't like either choice this time around, so I just didn't vote."

"That *is* a vote, Gayle," Peggy said. "Not voting *is* a vote. You know what an awful mess he made of things. And more and more is coming out daily."

"Saying things you agreed with?" Bobby repeated. "Against immigrants? *Gays?*"

"It's done," Gayle said, signaling she didn't want to discuss it further.

"He wasn't for anyone but himself," Val added. "And taking

away the rights of others."

"We are more than a year past the election. What could you have possibly done to anger her at this point?" Bobby asked Mike sincerely.

"I'm warning you, it's a long-ass story," Mike said. "I'll tell you, but you need to know everything."

"I'm not leaving until I hear it all," Val said, with Char nodding in agreement.

"Same," Bobby and Karen replied in unison.

"I'll lock the damn door if you try to leave now," Peggy added in a tone that made me realize she was serious. "And Maggie darling, you can stay or go. It's up to you."

"I'll stay," she said.

All eyes were on Mike. I already knew how hurt he was by all of this. How he kept thinking he was to blame. I had assured him that wasn't true. It was just a bad situation all the way around.

CHAPTER

Since there were so few customers in the bar, Peggy had moved a table from another booth and butted it up to the table in the booth where we were seated.

"Swap places with me," Peggy instructed Mike, "So everyone can see you better."

Once Mike was at the head of the long table, and Peggy was seated beside me, he began.

"As most of you know, I've been guilty of posting political memes and such on social media for the last several years. For the most part, I've tried to post only facts. You know, things that were said and then denied. And as you also know, some people don't want to hear facts."

"Connie rarely posted anything political, although she was

always quick to 'like' a comment that I adamantly disagreed with. You know, something posted by mutual friends or classmates," Mike continued. "I learned early on not to comment on things I didn't like or knew to be false. It had become clear that you couldn't change someone's opinion on social media."

"You made a good point, and I realize now that I was wrong is not something you ever hear anyone say," Val added with a smile.

"Exactly," confirmed Char.

"I know I've lost a few friends over politics – whether their choice or mine," Mike admitted. "But when you've seen that side of someone, especially if it's something that impacts you, then I question if we even need to be friends."

"But that's not what happened with Connie, is it?" Gayle asked with concern.

"No, and I'm still friends with people who think differently than me," Mike confessed. "I respect a difference of opinion, but I also find it's best not to discuss certain things. Basically, that's how I felt with Connie."

"But?" Val asked, leaning forward.

"Connie had always been one of the first to 'like' a comment, photo or meme on my page. And, if it was something personal that I had shared, she'd comment," Mike continued. "A while back, that stopped. She didn't unfriend me or block me, but I believe she chose to unfollow me."

"So she wouldn't see what's going on in your life, good or bad?" Bobby commented. "In other words, she was no longer interested in knowing anything about you."

"That's how it felt," Mike replied. "I thought after the election it might change because I rarely post anything political now."

"But she wouldn't know that since she doesn't follow you," Maggie added.

"What about you, Gayle? Have you unfollowed Mike?" asked Val.

"I have an account, but I don't post or comment," Gayle explained. "I'm more of a voyeur, a peeping Tom like Ricky's friend. I try to stay clear of conflict."

"Whereas Mike's a drama magnet," I added for levity.

"So, if Connie doesn't follow you, then how did you piss her off?" asked Peggy.

"Again, you're assuming I'm at fault," Mike replied.

Peggy shrugged.

"Most of you know or have heard me talk about Ming," Mike began. "To bring you up to speed, Maggie, I have worked with Ming for many years. She fabricates window treatments, bedspreads and pillows for my design clients."

"She made my draperies when Mike helped me redecorate," Gayle added.

"She worked briefly in my mom's design business back in the 1980s," Val shared. "Needless to say, her personality and my mom's did not gel."

"She *is* an acquired taste," Gayle remarked, leaning back in her chair.

"Is she Asian?" Maggie asked. "Ming is such an unusual name."

"Hell, no," answered Val laughing. "It's Ming Leatherwood. Doesn't that just roll off of your tongue?"

"Let's just say she isn't as exotic as her first name implies," Gayle inserted.

"Anyway, Ming and her husband Gator have worked with me on numerous projects over the years."

"Wait a second," Peggy interrupted. "Gator? His name is Gator Leatherwood?"

"It's a nickname, although I'm not sure how it came to be," Mike explained.

"Is Ming a nickname, too?" Maggie asked while adjusting her ponytail.

"Surely that's not her real name," Karen said, adding, "Is it?"

"Ming the Merciless from the old *Flash Gordon* comic strip," I suggested with a smile.

Mike sat there silently debating how much he was going to reveal.

"I can't really say," he finally admitted.

"Can't say if it's a nickname – or can't say what her real name is?" asked Peggy.

"Okay, Ming is not her real name, but it's the name she goes by," Mike shared. "Her real name is a little more southern."

"More compatible with Gator?" Karen joked.

"Yes." Mike leaned forward to whisper. "Something similar to Nancy Lou, Linda Sue, or Betty Ann."

"But she sees herself as a 'Ming'?" Maggie asked. "Nothing wrong with that."

I agreed. We all see ourselves differently than others might. Why not try and become that person? After all, in another life, I thought of myself as Nathaniel.

"What do Ming and Gator have to do with you and Connie?" Peggy asked, wanting to move the story along.

"Ming and Gator drank the Kool-aid, in fact bathed in it, with the last President," Mike answered. "Ming more so than Gator. We couldn't mention one thing politically without it escalating into an argument. If I said anything, she'd respond with what she had to endure the eight years before her guy came into office."

"Endure?" Bobby repeated, looking surprised. "Seriously, I wish he was back in office. At least he could string words together into a complete sentence."

"Ming would often accompany me to trade shows. She could be lots of fun and make the long drives bearable. We're alike in so many ways."

"Exactly," I added, nodding.

"But if anyone said anything negative about *her* President, she'd go ballistic," Mike continued. "Or if she found someone she felt was a kindred spirit, they would gang up on me. More and more uncomfortable situations arose until I finally stopped going so I wouldn't have to take her."

"And Gator was the same?" Maggie asked.

"Not as much," Mike revealed. "He worshiped her. Even left his wife and kid for her. It wasn't that he was a wimp or anything, he just knew it was easier to agree with her than to argue."

"I can see that," Gayle added. "She kind of intimidated me. I didn't want to say anything since she worked for you and was your friend, but she could be scary. The way she'd snap at Gator during an installation made me embarrassed for him."

"Her strong personality up against my mom's was frightening to watch," Val confessed, responding to Gayle's comment. "But my mom stood strong. I remember her telling Ming that it was *her* design business, *her* clients, and that it would be done *her* way. That was when Ming quit."

"Been there," Mike admitted. "I'd meet with my client, make my proposal and hire Ming to do the work. She'd then tell me how *she* thought it should be. I'd hold my ground, and she'd eventually do as I asked. But by then, my stomach would be in knots."

"I can remember you calling me after one of your showdowns," I added. "And what did I always tell you?"

"To fire her ass," Mike replied.

"This is all very interesting, but I still don't know what it has to do with Connie," Peggy stated.

"Ming and Gator came by Mike's house to drop off some throw pillows for a client," I explained for Mike. "Ming mentioned the two of them having colds. Mike didn't think anything of it at the time."

"Oh, no," Karen said, realizing where this was headed. "Were they wearing masks?"

"No. I checked on her a couple of days later. You know, wondering how they were feeling," Mike revealed. "But she didn't reply. I tried again the next day. I did this thing that she'd always do to me if I didn't respond in what she'd consider a timely matter. I sent a text with only a question mark. She texted back with one word – better. That's when I knew something was wrong."

"Ooh, nothing but a question mark? It's like those people

who text back 'K' instead of okay," Val inserted. "As if they are too busy to type anything else."

"COVID?" Maggie asked.

Mike shared that he checked their social media pages, and neither had been on for several days. This not only concerned him but alarmed him. They live north of Bellwood in the next county. He called the hospital there and asked for Ming's room. He was relieved when they said they didn't have a patient by that name.

"I'm surprised the hospital would reveal anything," Bobby said.

"That's why I asked to be connected to their room," Mike explained. "I figured they'd either connect me or say they don't have a patient by that name – which was Ming's case."

"But they told you about Gator?" Val asked to clarify.

"Yes, and they said he was in the ICU," Mike shared. "I was worried, assuming neither had been vaccinated. At our age, I feared the worst. In fact, Gator was three or four years older than me."

"My age," Peggy reminded us.

"I'd call the hospital daily to ask and was told the same

thing. Ming had yet to reply to my texts or answer my calls. Two weeks later, I got a different answer when I called the hospital. I was told to contact a family member," Mike revealed. "That's when I realized Gator must have died."

"That's awful," said Gayle. "He was so sweet, very laid back and chill compared to his wife. Plus, he had that great dry sense of humor."

"I remember you making a post about his passing," Karen remarked. "Ming had made draperies for me, but I wasn't home when they were installed. I never had the chance to meet them."

"I contacted a mutual friend to make sure she knew about Gator. Victoria's a design rep and said Ming had confided in her from the start," Mike added. "She showed me Ming's texts talking about shopping and picking up dinner – saying it about wore her out. It was clear that Ming never quarantined as recommended."

"Out infecting others," Maggie stated.

"Another text mentioned having friends over. She went on and on about the disposal getting clogged," Mike shared.

"Nothing about her husband in the hospital?" Peggy asked.

"A very brief mention," Mike replied. "Almost as an afterthought."

"Wait a second," Val said, sitting up straight. "She told this mutual friend all of this, plus that they had COVID, but didn't tell you? Never told you that they might have infected you? And, in turn, you could have given it to someone else?"

"Never checked on you to see if you were okay?" Char asked, picking up from where Val left off. "She didn't know one way or another if she had endangered you."

"And there you have it," I stated. "It was a senseless death, and I'm sorry. Mike had been her friend and worked with her for years, but she didn't care enough to tell him they had COVID. Or that Gator had died."

"Although she did tell the friend you mentioned," Maggie reminded us. "So it wasn't like she was keeping it a secret. She just didn't think you deserved to know."

Peggy tapped her nose, acknowledging that Maggie was correct.

"A client reached out to me to say how sorry she was that Gator had died. I asked how she knew, and she explained that she had read it on a friend's social media page," Mike revealed.

"She gave me that person's name. I found their post and then shared it to my page. I thought my clients would want to know."

"Understandably," Bobby said.

"Gayle, do you remember Jackie Prince?" Mike asked. "She didn't go to school with us, but lived in the neighborhood and was friends with many of our classmates."

"I do. She was always a little..." Gayle hesitated, "off, wasn't she?"

"That's putting it mildly," Mike said. "There's not a conspiracy theory out there that she doesn't believe. She's also against the vaccine and touts that horse dewormer medicine. She'll make some off-the-wall post to stir things up, followed with 'and that's all I'm going to say about it.' One of the last things I saw her post was about tunnels under Walmart for trafficking children."

"Jeez," Peggy uttered. "She really is nuts."

Mike went on to explain that he had done work for Jackie in the past, including having Ming make draperies and a bedspread – which was how Jackie met Ming.

"Jackie and I had a falling out when I made the mistake of posting facts after one of her bogus claims," Mike shared.

"She responded by sending me a private message saying that she now looks around her house at the beautiful touches I added and that all they remind her of is how much I hate her."

"Seriously?" Gayle asked.

"Yes. I never responded."

"As you said earlier, people don't want facts that contradict their beliefs," Val added, leaning back into the booth.

"I hate to sound like a broken record, but what does this Jackie, Ming and Gator have to do with you and Connie?" Peggy asked with frustration.

"He told you it was a long-ass story," I reminded her.

"Go on, Mike," Karen encouraged, smiling.

I looked around the bar and counted only seven customers and one bartender. It appeared that Maggie was the sole waitperson and not needed at the moment. My thoughts drifted to what Mike and I could do to renovate this space into a classic piano bar and cocktail lounge. I wondered once the changes were done, would there be an appeal? Would the crowd pick back up?

"I got a message from Jackie that said Ming was furious

that I had announced Gator's death before she did," Mike said.

"Ming hadn't posted anything?" Val asked. "Or, had someone post about his passing?"

"Not until several days later," Mike answered. "Jackie said Ming had asked me not to post, which was a lie. At that time, I hadn't heard, and still haven't heard, from Ming. I told Jackie that Gator's death should be a wakeup call for Ming *and* for herself to quit deworming and get vaccinated."

"Love it," Karen remarked. "What was her response?"

"Just like Ming, nothing," Mike replied. "After a couple more weeks, I decided I no longer wanted to work with Ming. However, I still had several things at my house that I had tried to sell for her – a coverlet, shams, and a few throw pillows. I sent an email that I carefully revised numerous times, knowing others might read it. I talked about the good times, all of the things she had done or helped with over the years. I told her sincerely how much I had liked Gator and respected him. But I added that I couldn't continue working with her. The fact that she thought so little of me and our friendship that she didn't let me know Gator was in the hospital or that he had died. And bottom line, that she didn't care enough to check to see if she had infected me."

"Plus, you asked her to pick up her things," I reminded Mike.

"Yes. But I said when the time was right I'd appreciate it if she'd send someone by to pick them up."

"Did she get back with you?" Gayle asked.

"It took a couple of days before I received her ridiculous reply, saying she had already asked someone last week to pick up her things – get this – next week."

"Really?" Karen asked. "She asked someone last week to pick up her things in two weeks? I'm not buying it. She just wanted to act like it was her idea and not yours."

"I didn't call her out on it," Mike shared. "I knew she was lying. And she had to know that I knew she was lying. When she finally posted online about Gator's death, she began with something like 'other people felt the need to post this before me' and then went on to mention the people Gator had left behind, with the exception of his son."

"Why?" Gayle asked.

"I don't know – other than I think his son had borrowed

money from them at one time and didn't pay it back," Mike answered.

"That still doesn't change the fact he was Gator's son," Val said. "How petty."

"I'll tell you the epitome of petty," I began with a raised voice. "Friends were writing condolences on her post, and Mike did the same. But she deleted it."

"It's true. I went back later to see who else had posted and what they had to say about Gator," Mike explained. "That's when I realized my post was gone. I posted it again, and less than thirty minutes later, it had been deleted."

"Her husband had just died, and still she had time to check to see if you posted something nice, and she deleted it?" Karen said. "She needs help."

"What about Connie?" Peggy asked impatiently.

"An artisan I had worked with over the years called to say he was in town and wanted to drop by," Mike explained. "I sold his framed mirrors and looked forward to seeing him. We set a time to get together, and visited for about an hour, but eventually, we ran out of things to talk about. And still, he lingered. I assumed he was killing time."

"Is that Danny? I can't remember – did he know Ming?" Bobby asked.

"Yes, and yes," Mike answered. "I had sold several of his mirrors, and Ming had commissioned him to do a matching pair for her bathroom. I had some of his mirrors still in my inventory."

"Did he know about Gator?" Peggy asked. "About your falling out with Ming?"

"Yes," Mike confirmed. "He kept wanting to talk about it. Wanted to know how I felt about it. Did I have anyone to replace her? He had never been that chatty or inquisitive in the past, so it seemed out of character."

"Pumping you for information?" Maggie asked.

"That's what it felt like. And then, the doorbell rang," Mike said, continuing his story. "It was Connie."

"Finally," remarked Peggy looking around the table.

"Behind her walking up the sidewalk was Jackie," Mike revealed. "And that's when I knew."

"She was there to pick up for Ming?" Val asked in disbelief.

"I asked Connie, and she quickly said that she didn't want to be put in the middle," Mike shared.

"But she was in the middle," Peggy remarked. "She put herself there or let herself be put in the middle."

"Connie told me that she had checked on Ming after Gator died and asked if there was anything she could do," Mike shared.

"That sounds like Connie," Gayle added.

"True," Mike agreed. "She said Ming asked her to pick up her things from me, and she felt she couldn't say no. However, she wasn't the one who actually picked up the inventory. It was Jackie who barged into my home like a freight train demanding to know where Ming's things were. I took her upstairs and showed her the pile of pillows and bedspreads."

"What about Danny?" Bobby asked.

"I'd already forgotten about him," Karen said.

"He was still there, lurking in the shadows, observing," Mike explained. "I expected him to start taking notes."

"Creepy," Gayle commented.

"As Jackie loaded up the car, Connie said again that she didn't want to be put in the middle," Mike continued. "I warned her that she was running around with two unvaccinated women and that she needed to be careful."

"Isn't Connie vaccinated?" Char asked Gayle.

"Yes, with her husband's health issues and grand-children, she has to be," Gayle explained.

"This is what I thought was odd..." Mike began.

"Everything about this is odd," Peggy mumbled.

"Connie said she was being careful. She added that she even drove alone in her car," Mike shared.

"Then what did she say?" Gayle asked, shifting in her chair.

"That she wasn't going with them," Mike replied. "Connie had simply driven to my house to be there when Jackie picked up. She wasn't needed and didn't load the first thing. There was absolutely no reason for her to come."

"Except to be a slap in your face," I said, with everyone nodding. "Out of all of Ming's friends, she asks *your* friend of fifty years to do this. It was all about control. And either Connie fell for it or chose to go along with it."

"Oh, and get this. Connie said that Ming told her that she never had COVID and that she wasn't even sure Gator had it," Mike added. "I asked Victoria if that's what she'd been told, and she said no. She then reminded me of Ming's texts where she talked about both of them testing positive for COVID. And that they had even gone for the Monoclonal Antibody Infusion."

"Is there or was there a memorial service of some kind for Gator?" Gayle asked.

"Not that I'm aware of," Mike answered.

"And this is why Connie's not here?" Peggy asked. "She thinks you're upset with her?"

"I *am* upset with her," Mike admitted. "Even if we buy that she got stuck in the middle of our drama and couldn't see a way out, she could have called ahead of time and given me a heads up instead of blindsiding me with a surprise ambush."

"And she could have warned you about Jackie," I added.

"You could have put Ming's things on the porch if you had known," Val said. "And kept that anti-vaxxer friend of hers out of your house."

"Did you tell Connie that?" Gayle asked.

"No, I care too much about her to tell her how she had hurt me," Mike said.

"Now that we know about Connie, I'm curious about this Danny fellow," Peggy remarked.

"I've got this," I said to Mike. "After Jackie and Connie had gone, Danny still hung around asking questions – wanting Mike to talk about it. Mike said the hairs on the back of his neck were at attention, so he didn't say anything negative. Only that it had been a long time coming and that he wished Ming all the best."

"You're a better man than me," Bobby said to Mike.

"Danny told Mike that Jackie had liked one of his mirrors – had mentioned it to him when Mike and Connie were talking," I continued. "Mike told him he was sorry but that Jackie wouldn't be back and wouldn't be buying it. He assured Danny that he would get it sold."

"Why do I feel like there is more?" Karen asked.

"Two days later, Danny, on his way back out of town, stops in and says he had a show coming up and needed inventory. He asked if he could pick up at least one mirror to help fill in," I explained.

"He didn't?" Maggie asked.

"Didn't what?" Bobby questioned.

"He did!" I exclaimed. "He wanted to pick up the same mirror that Jackie liked. Mike can't prove it but, he assumes Danny sold it to her directly."

"Would he even know how to get in touch with her?" Val asked.

"I doubt it. But I imagine Ming would have been happy to broker the deal for him," Mike said.

"That shit!" Peggy exclaimed.

"We don't know for sure but it does seems likely," Mike said.

"Well, we're 99.9% sure," I added. "Mike contacted Danny several days later and told him one of his customers had asked if it was still available."

"Is that true?" Char asked.

"Of course not," I admitted. "But when Mike asked Danny about it, he told him it had been sold."

"I remarked that I thought his show wasn't until next month," Mike added. "Danny confirmed that it was, but that someone had stopped by his studio and just had to have it."

"My, that's one hell of a popular mirror," Peggy said sarcastically.

"So this whole thing was orchestrated," Char surmised. "Danny comes to town and sets an appointment with you. He hangs around until Connie and Jackie show up and doesn't leave until after they have left. He pumps you for information and then comes back a couple of days later to pick up the one mirror that Ming's friend, the deworming queen Jackie, wanted."

"Wait, there's more," I announced. "Ming has now blocked Mike from all of her social media. But his friend Victoria shared one of Ming's posts with him. There are photos of Danny's mirrors on Ming's page announcing that her 'dear friend Danny' was now represented through a different design shop."

"First Connie and then Danny," Karen said. "It's like a divorce where friends have to choose sides. She's playing a game, thinking it will upset you. It's like she's saying: your friends have chosen me."

"And now your mirror guy doesn't need you anymore because he has another outlet," Bobby added.

"There are other mirror vendors out there if I need one," Mike said. "Plus, I'm not actively looking for clients."

"I think we should keep this conversation to ourselves," I suggested. "After all, it's between Mike and Connie and will only get more complicated if we get involved and misspeak for either of them."

"I agree," Peggy added. "Except, I still don't know why Connie isn't here tonight. Or why she said to ask Mike."

"Maybe she finally realized that she mishandled it," Karen said.

"Or Ming told her something untrue about Mike," Val added. "I have no problem imagining Ming spreading lies."

"When Victoria shared Ming's post about Danny, she said Ming had told her not to tell Mike," I explained. "Ming accused Mike of stalking her and others – said several of his clients had confided how uncomfortable they were around him."

"That's bullshit!" snapped Bobby.

Karen asked, "Do you trust Victoria to be honest with you?"

"I've worked with her for years," Mike explained. "And since Ming didn't work exclusively for me, there were times that Victoria sold to her as well. And I know that they have done some things socially over the years."

"But do you trust her?" Karen repeated her question.

"I do," Mike replied. "One, she got fed up with Ming's cavalier attitude when Gator was in the hospital. She was shocked that Ming was out shopping and having friends over instead of quarantining. As I said earlier, Victoria shared screenshots with me of Ming's texts."

"Still, there's more to the story of Connie's absence tonight," Char said. "What do you think, Mike?"

"I think that I'm disappointed. But, I also know what a manipulator Ming can be. Now that I've stepped back from our friendship, I can see it more clearly," Mike confessed.

After a bathroom break and a much-needed stretching of our legs, we sat back down. I had hoped the conversation would go in a different direction, but that was not the case.

"What am I supposed to tell Connie?" Gayle asked. "She will want to know what was said tonight."

"Gayle, I don't want you to get in the middle of this either," Mike said.

"You mean like Connie got in the middle of it?" Bobby reminded everyone.

"Seriously, guys, this is between Ming and Mike," Val began. "It's not our place to butt in."

"And when did that stop any of us?" Peggy asked in a sarcastic tone.

"Maybe she'll open up to you, Gayle, and we can find out

what her real problem is," Char added.

"I know I'm just the waitress here," Maggie began, "but it *is* an issue between Mike and this Ming character. Connie isn't a part of it, shouldn't be a part of it, and shouldn't have a say in it."

Everyone sat in silence for a minute before Bobby chimed in saying, "Yes! I second that! My thoughts exactly."

"Thanks, but can I just say that I'm tired of talking about Ming? Tired of hearing her fake name. Tired of worrying about Connie's feelings. Tired of feeling hurt by both of them," Mike said in frustration. "It's sad. I've not only lost a friend in Gator, but I've lost a friendship with Ming."

"Then time to move on," Peggy announced. "Enough about you, let's talk about me. And how you guys are going to turn this dump into an intimate, sexy, and welcoming piano bar."

"First, I have questions," Gayle blurted out. "Do you have a piano? You know that it needs to be a baby grand."

"Ebony baby grand," I clarified, as Gayle nodded.

"And do you have a piano player? Several, I would think," she continued.

"Several?" asked Maggie. "Why?"

"What if it's Friday night, the bar is packed, and the pianist calls in sick?" Gayle explained.

"She's got a point," Karen added. "Or a relative dies, and he needs to go out of town?"

"He?" asked Val. "There are women who know how to play piano."

"And *he* needs to be able to play by ear," Bobby added. "Sheet music is okay, but if someone tips for a special request, and he doesn't have the music, then he needs to be able to fake it."

"We have a few leads, all male, by the way," Maggie said, adding, "sorry, Val."

"But, we're flexible," Peggy said.

"So was I, forty years ago," I added for a laugh.

Peggy explained that she had her eye on a used five-foot-eight ebony grand at the local piano store that someone had traded in for an upgrade. She also shared that both the salesman and the owner were gay, loved the idea of a piano bar, and had made her a really good deal. Plus, the salesman wanted to audition for the job.

"He was really cute if you're into that sort of thing," Maggie explained. "And very personable."

"Single?" Bobby asked.

"I don't know if Victor is in a relationship or not," added Maggie.

"Victor?" Bobby asked. "I had a few dates with a Victor recently."

"This couldn't be the same Victor," Peggy said. "He's probably still in his twenties."

"Dark hair and eyes with a megawatt smile," Maggie began to describe. "Oh, and a goatee."

All eyes turned to Bobby, who sheepishly added: "And a tattoo band around his left bicep."

"Uh-oh," Val uttered. "So, daddy – I mean, Bobby – any other distinguishing marks?"

"Do we need to ask him to strip for the audition?" Peggy joked.

"Is that an option?" I lustfully asked.

"Bottom line, any guy *or* gal you hire is bound to have past relationships, good and bad," Char inserted as a voice of reason. "Bobby, how did your affair end?"

"It wasn't an affair. Just a couple of dates," he answered.

"I had one of those slap-across-the-face wake-up calls when Victor talked about the surprise birthday party his mom and he were throwing for his dad's sixtieth birthday."

"Sixtieth?" I asked. "Victor's dad is younger than you?"

"Ouch," Karen said, patting Bobby's hand.

"Did you consider asking his dad out?" Mike asked, snickering.

We were all laughing hysterically when the jukebox came to life. I had watched the bartender walk over, put money in, and make his selection. It was like the heavens opened up, and an angel started to sing. The one and only Miss Dolly Parton began to sing her heartfelt hit from 1974 – the same year that I, along with Mike, Karen, Gayle, and our dear friend Dean graduated college. A lifetime ago – forty-seven years to be exact.

Dolly began to speak the verse where she says she hopes life treats us kind and that we have all that we ever dreamed of. Then, with Dean in our hearts, we sang "I Will Always Love You."

When the song ended, Val repeated what she has said time and time again through the years. "Who doesn't love Dolly?"

"Wow, on that note, I think I'm going to say goodnight," Karen announced as she started to stand.

"Hold up a minute," Peggy said, turning to me. "How long are you staying in town?"

"I'm not on any schedule, but I had thought about going home Wednesday," I answered.

"Then I suggest we get together again Tuesday," Peggy continued. "One, I want to know what excuse Connie offered. Better yet, have her come tell us what's going on. And two, like Karen suggested, I'd like for you to tell us about your friend Jim."

"I'd like that, too," added Bobby.

"I'm game," said Gayle. "And, I'll let you know what's up after I talk with Connie. I'll strongly encourage her to join us. I don't like any of us being at odds with each other."

"We're in," answered Val as Char nodded.

"I'm curious about Connie, but I really want to know about your friend, Jim," Maggie said. "I'll admit that I was fascinated by his book. Yours too."

"You've read my book?" I asked. "Anyone else?"

"We all have, you fruitcake," Val added. "You're family."

I felt my heart swell. And at the same time, I missed my "family" of friends in Hillmont. I wondered if we'd ever come back together again.

—•—

"The family remark got to you, didn't it?" Mike asked on the drive back to his place.

"It did, but for several reasons," I admitted.

I reminded him how close we were back in the Nathaniel days – fearless – thinking things would never change. Some of us moved in and out of relationships, but we still remained friends. Although there were some relationships that exploded, and no one could put the pieces back together again. Bottom line, my Nathaniel family was no more.

However, a new family came together with my Hillmont friends. The love and bond I felt with Jim and Jeff. The joy in witnessing Diana's sassiness as she and Jim had tangled in their love/hate friendship. It was pure entertainment to watch the two of them go at it. I know it shocked Diana that, after all of her years in law enforcement, she could become best friends with someone who, in her past, she'd gladly arrest.

And Dylan. Poor vulnerable Dylan. What a tragic life he had until Jim and Jeff, who thought of him as a son, convinced him that he was worthy of being loved. Then, he lost both of them in such a short period of time. Heartbreaking. Although he has found love with Trevor, I continue to worry about him.

Plus, my long-time friend, dear Roberta Ann. I can only imagine the nightmares she still has from being the one to find Jim after his murderer's hate-filled attack.

"Ricky?" Mike asked. "Did I lose you again?"

"I'm sorry," I began. "It's just that..."

"I know," Mike said. "I miss them, too."

I reached over and ran my hand through his hair and down his cheek.

"Have you ever thought about how we came to be?" I asked. "Dean was our connection – the crossover between Bellwood and Hillmont. And now it's us. You and your Bellwood family and me and my Hillmont family."

"You don't have to talk about it Tuesday," Mike continued. "You don't owe anyone an explanation."

"I know," I said. "But maybe it will be cathartic."

"You do realize that Val didn't mean what she said about Jim," Mike added.

"She did," I contradicted. "But that's because she doesn't know the whole story. She only knows the Jim who wrote the book."

"True."

We were now back at Mike's home, the same 1960s ranch-style house he and Bobby shared many years ago. Of course, Mike had redecorated and updated it time and time again, and it was stunning. The screened-in porch was still one of my favorite areas. His design studio was above the garage, and I wondered why he never relocated to a commercial space somewhere. But Mike was not quick to make changes. He was always comfortable working from home.

"What are you thinking about?" he asked.

"Just wondering why you never moved your design studio to somewhere larger, more convenient for your clients – and private?" I shared.

"You worked out of your home for years." he countered. "Why didn't you?"

"I'm lazy," I joked.

"We both know that's a lie," he replied. "I will admit that you had a better arrangement with the business downstairs and your private quarters upstairs."

"Private quarters!" I repeated. "I like that. Speaking of which, are you going to show me your private quarters tonight?"

"You've seen it," Mike replied. "Are you feeling frisky, Nathaniel? Wanting to do a little midnight moving under the sheets?"

We both laughed at the thought as we got out of the car. And we both knew that neither of us had the energy to get anything started this late.

"Maybe in the morning," I suggested.

"Something to look forward to," Mike said, in a way that let me know he meant it.

CHAPTER

Three

On Saturday and Sunday, Mike and I fiddled-farted around, as my dad used to say. It's hard to believe that if he were still alive, he would have turned 100 on his last birthday. But a heart attack at seventy-eight kept that from happening. Remembering that I'm just nine years away from my seventy-eighth birthday caused a chill to go down my spine.

Mike and I were like an old married couple grocery shopping together and then riding around discussing all the changes taking place in Bellwood. Things like the craze of tearing down modest homes and replacing them with ostentatious monuments painted white that screamed "new money." We talked about going to a movie, but even though the theaters had reopened, neither of us felt comfortable with the idea.

Wearing a mask for a long time was uncomfortable. Granted, it was no longer required, but we preferred staying safe.

Monday morning, Mike was in his studio when I heard a stream of obscenities being spewed at top volume. I rushed up the stairs, afraid of what I'd find, but Mike was just sitting at his desk staring at his computer.

"What the hell, Mike?" I asked.

He waved me over and pointed to the screen. I wasn't sure what I was looking at, but as my eyes focused, I understood that it was an email forwarded to Mike that morning. I learned later that, it was one of more than a dozen.

"Ming's been busy," he said calmly. It appeared that Ming had sent an email to Mike's clients.

The email stated that since Mike "has retired" and is "no longer practicing design," she wanted to reach out to those whom she had worked with in the past and offer her "design" services. Ming even went so far as to say that by "cutting out the middle man" (Mike), she could offer much more competitive pricing for her services.

"You're officially retiring?" I asked already aware of the answer.

"No," he snarled. "You know I'm winding down, but I haven't made that known to clients. As soon as they hear you're retiring, they go elsewhere. I wanted it to be my decision."

"So, Ming just retired you?" I repeated. "She put it out there as fact, and now you start the denial. Basically, you have to prove that you're still going strong, or you're done."

"I have been taking on fewer clients and, as jobs concluded, not rushing to add another," Mike explained. "But I'm still working and had planned to continue working for at least another year or two."

"Did you ever tell Ming you planned to stop?" I asked.

"Sure," he said. "I've always talked about retiring at seventy. Ming's the same age and said she'd probably be ready by then as well."

"What the hell happened to make her so vindictive?" I asked. "She's put a target on your back."

"I still don't know," Mike answered, getting more and more frustrated. "You know that she won't talk to me."

I chose not to push anymore. I was furious too but realized Mike needed me to have a level head – to talk him off the ledge instead of giving him a reason to jump.

"Okay," I said calmly, "you need to send out an email to discredit her. It can't be spiteful, but it has to make it clear that you're not going anywhere and that you are the one who has the design experience."

"I'm not sure who she contacted. There have been jobs that she didn't work on. Jobs where her services weren't needed – like this one," Mike explained, pointing to one of the emails forwarded to him from a client. "How did she get their contact info?"

"What about Danny?" I asked. "Were there jobs he worked that she might not have?"

"Sure," Mike answered, still not catching on.

"And, if they're in this together, then he would have information that she didn't have and vice versa. Correct?" I asked.

"Yes," he answered as the lightbulb came on. "I'll need to send an email to everyone."

"I'm afraid so."

"I'll need your help composing it," Mike admitted.

"I can do that."

For the next hour or so, we worked on a letter to be sent

to Mike's clients. Occasionally I'd throw in a descriptive name for Ming, only to delete it a few seconds later. Not helpful, but liberating. It just felt good to call her every despicable thing I could think of.

Finally, we had something that we thought would work.

Dear _____

It has been my pleasure to work with you in the past or to be working with you now on your design needs. I've enjoyed our collaboration and have been proud, as I'm sure you are, of our accomplishments.

This morning I learned that one of my past associates had reached out to my client list with misinformation. On the off chance you received a confusing email from a former vendor, please allow me to set the record straight.

In the past, I have used the services of Ming's Fabrications. She might have made your draperies, bedspreads or throw pillows. And, as I'm sure many of you would agree, she is excellent at what she does. While I was the one who consulted with you and created your entire design concept, Ming executed my designs.

Like you, I'm confused by her email stating that I'm out of the design business. First of all, I hope you know that when that time comes, you will hear the news from me and not one of my subcontractors. I'm sure you also found it confusing that she misrepresented her qualifications, along with the offer to discount her prices, thereby making it appear that designers overcharge. I've always worked on a cost-plus scale, sharing with my clients the actual invoices that I receive.

I did sever my ties with Ming and her husband after they exposed me to COVID. I certainly didn't want to risk exposing you. After catching COVID, Ming's husband went into the hospital and died a few weeks later. It breaks my heart.

I can only imagine the pain and guilt that she must be experiencing. Therefore, I look at this incident as a lack of judgment in a time of grief.

I want to assure you that I am still available for all of your design needs. And I hope that you will join me in a prayer of healing for Ming and her stepson.

"I'm not sure what else needs to be said," I commented.

"Me, either," Mike agreed.

"We basically said her actions could be grief-based instead of the fact that she's a psychotic vindictive…"

"Ricky," Mike interrupted. "In spite of what has happened, she was a friend – a co-worker for many years. She had a big heart..."

"Black heart," I said, followed by, "sorry."

"I agree that she was a walking contradiction," Mike continued. "But, I always felt I had a kindred spirit in her. The ugliness didn't really begin to show until the last presidency. Things that she had been an advocate for fell by the wayside if 'her' president disagreed – like the protection of animals. She simply brushed it off, saying you take the good with the bad."

"How that man had so much power is a mystery to me. Like 'The Emperor's New Clothes.' Half of the country saw him naked..."

"That's not a visual I want," Mike said as if he was about to gag.

"But, as I was saying, the other half of the country would swear he was wearing the finest of clothing," I finished. "It made no sense, still doesn't make sense to me."

"He gave people the right to hate out loud in the sunlight instead of staying quiet in the shadows. He led by example with his name-calling and bullying."

"If that's how Ming feels, then does she agree with taking away LGBTQ protections?" I asked.

"She never said that but you do have to wonder," Mike replied. "Do you think Gayle feels that way? Or Connie?"

"I can't see how they would and still be friends with all of us," I answered.

"I just thought of something," Mike said excitedly. "Gayle and Connie."

"What about them?"

"They are former design clients," he announced as if I didn't know. "The email."

"They should have gotten an email," I said catching on. "Whatcha bet Connie already knew about it?"

"I'd hate to think that," Mike said. "But you could be right."

"Call Gayle and put her on speaker phone," I suggested.

When Gayle answered, she began by saying that she hadn't asked Connie yet about Tuesday night because Connie hadn't returned her phone call or text.

"That's strange," Mike remarked. "But that's not why we called."

"We?"

"Hey, Gayle, Mike's got you on speaker phone. I hope you don't mind," I said, jumping in.

"Of course not. What's up?" she asked.

"Have you looked at your email this morning?" Mike anxiously asked.

"No. Has something happened?"

"Can you look at it now?" I butted in.

"Sure, hold on," she replied. "I just turned the computer on. What am I looking for?"

"Do you have an email from Ming's Fabrications?" Mike asked.

"Uh, no, no, no – wait, yes, I do."

"Please open it and read it," I asked. "Others have forwarded their email to us so we pretty much know what it says."

"Give me a sec," she said. "What the hell?"

"Exactly," Mike practically shouted. "Ming has announced my retirement about two years early."

"Why?" Gayle asked, as perplexed as the rest of us.

"Who knows?" I replied. "It appears she sent it to all of Mike's clients – even ones she didn't work for."

"But how would she know who they were?" Gayle asked.

"Danny," Mike answered.

"A couple of people who forwarded Mike the message asking if it was true had hired Danny to do work for them," I explained. "But not Ming."

"You think Danny helped her do this? That he has it out for you, too?" Gayle asked. "What is it that they think you have done to them?"

"If only I knew," Mike said.

"Do you want me to see if Connie got one, too? Or are you assuming she did, or that she helped?" Gayle asked. "I'm saying right now that I can't believe she'd be in on this."

Mike told Gayle that he hoped he was wrong – that maybe Connie had innocently gotten wrapped up in something. Mike still wanted to believe Connie was his friend. I didn't feel the same. But then, I didn't know her as well.

"I'm going to call and tell her I got this email. I'll act like I haven't spoken with you," Gayle said. "She's my oldest friend. But she's acting squirrelly, and I want to know why."

"Are you going to pretend you believe it and are surprised that I didn't tell you?" Mike asked.

"I think that might work," Gayle replied. "Did you check with Karen? She should have gotten one, too."

"You're right," I said. "I'll call her on *my* phone while you're still on the line."

I called Karen, and like Gayle, she hadn't opened her email. When she did, she let out a stream of words that would make a sailor blush. Combinations of words that I needed to remember for future use. I had her on speaker phone so Gayle could hear her as well.

"Now what?" asked Karen.

"Tell her what I said," Gayle said loudly.

Mike revealed Gayle's plan for Connie. Karen offered to call since Connie and Gayle were childhood friends. But Gayle insisted that she needed to do it, and if Connie didn't answer, she'd get in her car and show up at her front door.

Karen asked Mike what he planned to do. He explained to both of them about the letter, and they asked that we read it to them.

"Well done," Gayle commented when Mike had finished. "You discredit her as a professional designer and make the lower cost thing sound like a scam."

"And, you don't call her out for the you-know-what that she is. You give her a pass because of her grief," Karen remarked.

"And he acknowledges her carelessness regarding COVID," I added.

"I approve," Gayle commented. "When are you sending it out? I only ask because I think it would be good if Connie had received your email before I called."

"I can do it right now," Mike said.

"Great. I'll let you know as soon as I talk with her. She can't keep avoiding me," Gayle announced. "Regardless, I'll see all of you on Tuesday."

"Take care, Gayle," Karen shouted, hoping Gayle would hear.

"Okay, we have a plan," I stated with enthusiasm. "Talk soon."

CHAPTER

Four

Tuesday night, the eight of us met at Charlie's. Peggy and Maggie had already pushed tables together to accommodate our group.

"Were you able to reach all of your clients and set them straight?" Peggy began.

"Yes," Mike answered, then added, "sort of."

"Uh-oh," Val whispered.

"It's not bad," Mike continued. "Most everyone responded to my email, thanking me for an explanation. Some said they didn't have any projects coming up, but if things changed, I'd be the first one they'd contact. There were a few I didn't hear back from, so I called. Most had either not opened their email, or it had gone into spam."

"Where Ming's email belongs," Karen inserted.

"One client seemed rather evasive," Mike added. "I was trying to justify her response, thinking maybe she felt uncomfortable being dragged into my drama."

"But?" asked Maggie.

"Then Victoria called Mike," I blurted out. "You know, Victoria is the fabric rep who Ming has kept in touch with."

"Yes. She called this afternoon, saying that there was something she thought I should know," Mike picked up where I left off. "Ming had just placed an order with her and couldn't wait to tell her the news."

"The news?" Val asked.

"The news of my retirement," Mike explained. "Along with the fact that Ming would be taking over my clients. And that the order she was placing was for one of my past customers."

"Do you know which one?" Gayle asked.

"Yes. Ming gave Victoria the name for the order," Mike continued. "The same woman who had been weird on the phone with me earlier."

I jumped in to add Ming had told Victoria that she and the client had a *long* lunch to discuss a new project. She kept saying how much fun it had been and how the woman was so relieved because she hadn't wanted to work with Mike again but didn't know who to call.

"And get this," Mike added, "Ming called Victoria thirty minutes later and asked her not to tell me about it – said she didn't want me to be hurt."

"Bullshit," Peggy snapped.

"You see what she's doing, don't you?" Char asked. "She tells this Victoria something juicy, knowing that she'll tell you. Then she sweetens the deal by asking her to keep it a secret – pretending she cares about your feelings."

"Exactly," I added. "She's playing a game, and only she knows the rules."

"And using your friend Victoria as one of her pawns," Maggie surmised.

"Still, we don't know why," I said. "Unless Connie revealed something to Gayle."

All eyes turned to Gayle, hoping for answers. She cleared her throat, brushed her hair behind an ear, and began.

"I called and then texted Connie with no response," Gayle began. "So I drove over to her house. The garage door was going up when I got there and Connie was backing out."

"What did you do?" Mike asked.

"I blocked her," Gayle admitted. "Put my car in park, got out, walked up to her car and tapped on the window. She lowered it and, in a bit of a panic, asked me to move. She said her daughter had called and needed her to come over immediately."

"Was something wrong?" I asked.

"I asked Connie, but she said she couldn't talk. Then she asked me again if I'd move my car," Gayle continued. "I hesitated until she finally promised to call me that night and explain."

"And did she?" Karen asked.

"Yes, and you're not going to like it," Gayle began. "Connie said that Ming had shared things Mike had supposedly said about her, as well as things about me. Ming said that Mike had spread lies about her and that he's not as sweet and kind as he appears. That Mike had a dark side."

Val and Char began to laugh at the thought. "Little Mary Sunshine Mike has a dark side?" Val repeated. "That's rich."

"What did she accuse me of saying?" Mike asked.

"I wrote things down so I wouldn't forget," Gayle added, taking out a slip of paper. "You said at one time that if you looked in the dictionary under dumb blonde, Connie's picture would be there."

"I never..." Mike stuttered.

"If Connie believes that, then maybe she *is* dumber than I thought," I blurted out before thinking.

"What else?" Mike asked.

"Supposedly, I'm stuck up and think that I'm better than everyone else," Gayle continued.

"That's Ming projecting," Peggy said. "She's jealous of you."

"Ming said Mike thinks that lesbians are a joke," Gayle read from her list. "She didn't elaborate."

"A joke?" Val responded, looking at Mike.

"She also said that you broke up Karen's marriage with Dean," Gayle continued.

"How?" Karen asked.

"That he paid that Tammy Lynn..."

"Cunt!" Char, Val, Bobby and Karen said in unison.

"Whoa," exclaimed Maggie. "What's that all about?"

"Tammy Lynn was my best friend," Karen began. "Her

nickname was TL, and someone added the 'C,' as in the c-word, when everything came to light."

"TLC admitted what she did," Char continued the story. "She was jealous of Karen's happiness, and because Mike had been involved with Dean when they were young, she wanted to prove to Karen that Dean was gay."

"She actually said she was doing me a favor," Karen explained. "She tried making passes at Dean, and when he didn't follow through, she assumed he was gay."

"In her mind, no straight man could resist her," Bobby added.

"Finally, she had her way with my baby brother," Peggy said remorsefully. "And the guilt weighed on him so much that it began his negative spiral."

"And I didn't help," Karen admitted.

"Don't," Bobby said. "Don't second guess. You did what felt right to you at the time. There was a lot that factored into the way things turned out."

"I'm sorry Ming has hurt you by bringing all of this up," Mike apologized with compassion.

"Damn," Val exclaimed. "Anything else?"

"She said Mike accused her of stealing from a client. He said he knew that it had happened before when she worked for Val's mom."

"Busted," Val said, pounding her fist on the table.

"So busted," agreed Char.

"In what way?" Maggie asked.

"I told you that Ming worked for my mom back in the eighties. And, that she fired her," Val reminded us. "Well, when she left, a few things were missing."

"Like that designer in your book, Ricky," Mike added.

"Ming denied it, and my mom couldn't prove it," Val continued. "But it got ugly."

"I didn't know anything about that," Mike admitted. "You never told me."

"Right," Val said with a smile. "That's how we know she's lying."

"Val's mom asked us never to mention it," Char explained. "She didn't want to mess with Ming, and she didn't want it out there that she had hired a thief. Plus, it was so long ago. Even when we realized you were working with her, we decided not to say anything."

"I'm so confused," Mike said.

"What they're saying is you didn't know and couldn't have found out to have mentioned it to her," Peggy said. "So we know she's lying about that, at least."

"At least?" I questioned. "Are you having doubts about the other stuff?"

"I didn't say those things," Mike pleaded. "I swear."

"But Connie believes it. Right?" I asked. "Ming has convinced her that Mike is evil?"

"There's one more thing," Gayle said.

"Of course, there is," I mumbled.

"Gator's indiscretion," Gayle said.

"Affair?" Karen asked. "With Mike?"

"No," Mike answered. "So she knows?"

"Yes," Gayle replied. "Gator did a death bed confession."

"What the hell are you two talking about?" snapped Peggy.

Mike began to explain that quite a few years ago, Gator was unfaithful to Ming. Mike believed it was a lapse in judgment by Gator and that he never strayed again. It happened when his son came to dinner with a new girlfriend. But his son had forgotten the one thing Ming had asked for – to pick up beer on the way over. The son goes back out to the store, but the girlfriend stays.

"Ming wanted Gator to get something out of the second refrigerator they kept downstairs in her workroom. Maybe the salad or something else – I forget," Mike added. "But then she told Gator to show the girlfriend her workroom. The two of them go downstairs while Ming stays upstairs in the kitchen."

"And the son had gone for beer," Val reminded us.

Gator said the girlfriend, who had not been around Ming before, was not used to her bossing Gator and his son around. When they were alone, she asked if he enjoyed a woman telling him what to do. Gator said he laughed, not knowing where the conversation was headed. Then the girlfriend said something like, if that's the case, then maybe she should boss him around.

"Is this about to get kinky?" Bobby asked in anticipation.

"The girlfriend told Gator to unzip his pants," Mike shared. "Gator said he was in shock, thought she was joking, and just shook his head. Then she moved in, unzipped and exposed him in a blink of an eye before dropping to her knees."

"Then what?" Maggie whispered.

"Then they went back upstairs, the son returned, and they sat down for dinner," Mike concluded.

"Shit!" Val exclaimed. "And Ming never knew?"

"I guess not until Gator realized he wasn't going to make it," Gayle surmised. "Ming must have asked if anyone else knew, and he said he told Mike."

"Why would Gator confide in you?" I asked. "I didn't think you were that close."

"I'm not sure Ming let Gator have that many friends," Mike explained. "Often, there were times she'd send him to install a project but not come along. She knew that I'd be there and that she wasn't needed. Gator and I had time alone, especially if the client wasn't home."

"You were his confidant," Maggie stated. "I'm sure he felt safe confiding in you."

"He was right," Gayle added. "After all, you've kept his secret until now."

"And he was probably wracked with guilt," I said, as Mike nodded.

"Can you imagine cheating on Ming?" Mike asked. "She would have castrated him if she had known."

"What about his son's girlfriend?" Char asked.

"Gator told me they broke up the next day and that the girlfriend told his son that she preferred someone older, more mature," Mike explained. "You know, someone like Bobby – a daddy figure."

"Bitch," Bobby, said laughing.

"Why couldn't Connie come and tell us this herself?" Mike asked Gayle.

"You're not going to like this either," Gayle continued. "She's uncomfortable in a gay bar."

"What?" Peggy asked in disbelief. "The same Connie who has been coming in here almost weekly with you guys for years? Who has waited on a table or two when we were crowded and short-staffed? The same Connie whose photo is on the wall over there laughing her ass off with friends?"

"Yes," Gayle said, shaking her head. "Ming has convinced her, along with the past President, that gays and lesbians are an abomination. That she is part of a superior race."

"Holy shit!" Bobby yelled. "What about Gayle, Karen, and Peggy, for Christ's sake? They aren't gay. They like cock!"

"Crass, but we get your point," Karen remarked.

"She said she'd pray for me," Gayle confided in us. "It's like Connie has joined a cult."

"Or been brainwashed," Char added.

"I'm so angry," I blurted out. "Pissed at Connie. Pissed at Ming, at Gator. Pissed at those in our fucking government thinking we're second-class citizens."

"Ricky," Char said calmly, "as bad as you think it is for us, we're not alone. What about Blacks, Asians, Muslims, Mexicans, and others who aren't white?"

"And our trans brothers and sisters?" Val added.

"I hate it when you're the voice of reason," I said.

"Seriously though, what is our country becoming?" Karen asked.

"I would never have thought Connie would go down the rabbit hole with the likes of them," Mike said. "I'm so sorry that I didn't cut ties with Ming a while back. Please forgive me."

"Nothing to forgive," Val stated. "We should have warned you about Ming years ago."

"It's not your fault," Peggy declared. "Crazy people are just crazy. And mean people are just mean. It doesn't matter what any of us do or how we react. They will still be crazy and mean."

"I'm exhausted," Karen announced. "I was looking forward to hearing about your friend Jim, but I don't know if I have the strength."

"It's okay," I replied. "I'm too emotional to get into it tonight. If Mike will have me, I think I'd like to stay a few days longer."

"I'd love that," Mike said, grinning. "Stay as long as you'd like."

"Then let me ask you this," Karen began, "Lunch at my place this Thursday? Since we all have flexible schedules, would that work? These chairs from the back hall are butt-busters, and I think we still have some long conversations ahead of us."

"Are you sure?" Peggy asked. "I'd be happy to bring something."

"Us, too," said Char.

"Count me in," Gayle added.

"Why don't you set the table and let us bring the food?" Bobby offered. "I'll coordinate it and even bring flowers."

"Wonderful," Karen replied, beaming. "What about one o'clock?"

CHAPTER
Five

Mike continued to do damage control on Wednesday. Since he had been blocked, he was unable to see Ming's social media pages. However, even though Ming and I had never friended each other, I could. I called Mike's friend Victoria to confirm that I had access to everything.

"Since you're 'friends' with the she-devil," I began, "I wanted to compare pages with you to find out if I'm seeing all of her posts or if they are being filtered."

Victoria scrolled through her computer while I did the same once I logged in to Mike's desktop. I was surprised – they were alike. I asked her if she was seeing a meme that Ming had posted that morning. We were both taken back by the content. It was a doctor and a patient, and the doctor said the diagnosis was sniffles. He then prescribed house arrest, forced vaccinations, economic collapse, and 24-hour government surveillance.

"Can you believe this shit?" Victoria asked. "Her husband died because they were too stubborn or stupid to get the vaccination. And now she's posting stuff like this that makes fun of it."

"If she has a heart, then it's a cold one," I remarked. "I know it's awful to say, but it feels like she doesn't care."

"She's too busy with her vendetta against Mike. Planning a coup to take over his business," Victoria commented. "It's like January 6th all over again."

"Connie, Mike's childhood friend, will probably be quoted after the fact saying that it was a peaceful protest. Just a regular group of tourists," I joked.

"Is this Connie with Ming in the Christmas post?" Victoria asked.

I quickly scrolled back and found a photo of the two of them at a restaurant. Ming had commented how much fun it was to be out with her dear friend Connie. Adding that Connie had given her a tin filled with her signature fudge that she makes each Christmas.

"That's just last month," I stated the obvious. "Right after Gator's death and before Ming's attack on Mike."

"So they're friends after all?" Victoria asked. "Speaking of which, her page only has 210 friends."

"It's hard to comprehend that she'd have any," I commented. "Hold on, Mike's right here. Let me ask him something."

"When did Connie and Jackie pick up Ming's shit?"

"Thursday, December seventeenth," Mike answered after looking at his calendar for the date of his appointment with Danny.

"This post with Connie is dated Tuesday, December twenty-second," I stated.

"I guess that explains why I didn't get fudge at Christmas," Mike said, trying to be funny. "At least Ming waited until after the holidays to enact her revenge."

"Victoria, are you still there?" I asked.

"Yes. I'm tempted not to place her fabric order. Or to try and hold it up, if possible," Victoria responded.

"I think it's best if you act like you're on her side," I suggested. "Maybe she'll tell you something that can be helpful."

"Okay," she replied. "I'll keep you posted."

"One more thing," I added before hanging up, "there's a comment where someone asked what happened to one of her earlier posts – wondering if it had been taken down. Ming replied that she'll send it in a private message, adding that they need to take back their country."

"I saw that," Victoria explained. "I've noticed that she'll put something out there and then delete it before it incites the masses. Either she has second thoughts, or she is signaling her troops. Anyway, she takes it down before too many have a chance to see it."

"I think we're giving her too much credit," I commented. "We're assuming she has a plan or the intelligence to pull off a takedown."

"I'll admit that I've never seen this side of her," Victoria began, "But what I have witnessed is enough to make me never want to cross her."

"I don't want you to do anything that you're not comfortable with," I stressed. "We'll get through this."

"She may scare me," Victoria admitted. "But I'm more scared of what she'll do if she's not stopped."

"Thank you," I said sincerely. "I appreciate that, and you know how much Mike appreciates you."

"He's a sweetheart. I'm willing to help any way that I can."

I filled Mike in on Victoria's portion of the phone call. Since I was still logged in to his computer, he could see what we had discussed. When he refreshed the page, the doctor and the patient meme had already been deleted.

"Gator died near the end of November after confessing to his blow job. That resulted in Ming getting upset with me," Mike summarized.

"Blaming you and not her own husband," I clarified.

"I cut ties with Ming a couple of weeks later, and she sends Connie and Jackie to pick up her things, knowing that Danny would be at my house," Mike continued. "The next day she announces Danny has his stuff at another design studio. Then a few days later, she posts a photo of her and Connie exchanging Christmas gifts."

"I just scrolled through Connie's page and saw that she didn't share that photo. That's why none of you knew about her connection to Ming earlier."

"And, now we're into January, and Ming has gathered her

troops and gone to war," Mike remarked.

"None of it is making any sense," I confirmed.

Bobby called later about our luncheon at Karen's home. Maggie was bringing the entree – some kind of chicken dish. Peggy was in charge of bread. Val and Char opted for a vegetable, which left the salad and dessert for us. Mike said that he didn't care, so Bobby chose dessert, leaving us to prepare a salad.

"It just so happens I can rock a tasty salad," I told Mike. "You do what you need to do, and I'll handle the food."

"Thank you," he said with a half-smile. "I'm mentally exhausted and not sure I could focus on the ingredients."

"Not a problem," I assured him. "I'm going to the store and won't be gone long."

—●—

Everyone arrived promptly the following day for our get-together at Karen's. She not only had the table ready but had also whipped up some appetizers. While the chicken, vegetables, and rolls warmed in the oven, we sat down with our drinks and munched on Karen's offerings.

Karen's home was inviting, feminine, but not too girly.

Mike had helped her start over after the last divorce and had continued to freshen it up through the years. We were seated in her den. The grasscloth-covered walls had been painted in a calming pale blue-gray shade. The upholstery was a mixture of neutral textures such as linen, chenille and velvet.

Karen began, "I thought we could hear Jim's story during lunch. But first, is there anything new on the Ming/Connie fiasco?"

"Needless to say, I didn't invite Connie today," Gayle began. "It kills me to have this rift going. I keep asking myself, how did I not see her slipping into the abyss? When did Ming take my place?"

"Did she ever mention Ming before this?" Peggy asked. "Did you suspect anything?"

"No, but there is one thing that I thought of," Gayle answered. "Connie loves to play Scrabble online. And that Words with Friends game. She tried unsuccessfully to get me interested. I know that she plays with others and wondered if that was something Ming also enjoyed."

"I think that she does," Mike said. "I'm not sure which

game, but I remember her saying she plays something online with friends."

"I don't know how it would have started or when," Val commented, "but that could be what has kept them connected."

"It's all speculation at this point," Char added. "Right now, it feels like we need to plan an intervention for Connie."

"Do you know anything else about her daughter?" Karen asked Gayle. "You mentioned Connie was in a hurry to go see her. Was that just an excuse, or do you think something was wrong?"

"I'm such a bad friend. When Connie called, we immediately got into discussing Ming and Mike. I forgot to ask her anything about Sara – that's her name," Gayle said, turning to Maggie. "She's married and has a daughter, Connie's granddaughter."

I jumped into the conversation, sharing my phone call with Victoria.

"She really posted that meme?" Val asked. "That's as tasteless as her wardrobe of animal prints."

"Stop," Mike said, laughing. "I can't tell you how often clients would ask me if everything Ming owned was an animal print."

"Guys," Bobby said as everyone was getting rowdy with laughter. "Guys!"

"You don't have to yell," Peggy snapped.

"Clearly, I do," Bobby replied. "I just pulled up Ming's page out of curiosity, and this is her latest post. 'Big News Coming Soon.' Do you think the big news is her fantasy announcement of taking over, or taking down, your business?"

"I think I'm going to be sick," Mike said softly.

"Wait, there's more," Bobby continued. "She adds: 'thanks to all of my socialite friends for their support.' Who says that sort of thing? Seriously, would she even recognize a socialite?"

"The real question is whether any 'socialite' would recognize her," Val added, laughing.

"What else could it be?" Karen asked, laughing along. "Gayle? Did Connie say anything?"

"No. And I can't believe she'd be a part of this – unless she was convinced that Mike actually said he'd give Ming his business," Gayle replied. "The Connie I know wouldn't be part of something underhanded like that."

"You mean the Connie who will no longer set foot in a

gay bar?" Peggy asked.

"Scroll back to her December posts," I suggested.

Bobby did as I asked and then turned his phone for the others to see.

"So much for my hope that this was just a temporary lapse in judgment," Gayle said after seeing the photo of Connie and Ming together.

"Well, at least Ming only has 283 friends on her page," Bobby added.

"283?" I asked. "It was 210 yesterday. How could that be?"

"It's got to be some kind of mistake," Val said. "A glitch or something."

Karen thought we should take a break, clear our heads, stretch our legs, and step outside for some fresh air. Taking her suggestion, Bobby, Val and I stood on the front stoop. The sky was a clear blue, the sun was shining, and the temperature was in the high forties. A car passed by, followed by another. One more vehicle approached, going slower than the speed limit. Bobby and I weren't really paying attention until Val uttered: "Are you kidding me?"

Bobby and I quickly looked up to see it was a van with

Ming's Fabrications in bold letters painted on the right-side rear panel. And there, big as life, was Connie seated on the passenger's side, looking straight at us as it rolled by.

"I'm not imagining that, am I? Val asked. "I mean, we all saw that, right?"

"Come on," I said. "Let's go inside."

"You look like you've seen a ghost," Peggy exclaimed when we returned to the dining room.

"No, she was very much alive," Bobby said.

"Who was?" asked Gayle.

"Connie," I replied.

"What about Connie?" Gayle asked.

"She and Ming were out joy-riding in Ming's van," Bobby explained. "They drove in front of the house while we were standing there."

"You're making that up?" Gayle accused.

"No, they're not," Char said. "Val is speechless, which is next to impossible."

"Cute," Val responded in a tone that was anything but cute. "It was them. Ming's van. Connie, in the passenger seat staring at us."

"Was she in distress? Did she mouth 'help me?' Or did she look comfortable – like she belonged there?" Peggy asked.

"How would they even know that we're all here?" Karen wondered aloud. "I mean, it couldn't be a coincidence, could it? Surely they're not stalking my house."

Gayle went to retrieve her phone and began dialing. After a couple of seconds, she screamed: "What the hell, Connie? Do you have a death wish? You're in a closed-up van with an anti-vaxxer. Are you trying to get sick? Or are you being held hostage because that's what I'd prefer? At least I'd have a chance of rescuing you and getting you free from that lunatic."

"That's one hell of a message," Val said.

Karen put her arm around Gayle, allowing her to collapse against her. We felt helpless as we watched someone we cared about dive into the deep end of the pool, unable to swim.

"Come on, let's eat," Maggie said. "Sit down, and we'll try to figure it all out."

"I don't want to talk about it. I don't want to even think about it right now," Gayle announced. "I want to hear about Ricky's friend. I need to focus on something else. Can we do that?"

"Gayle, I'm happy to be a diversion, but my story isn't uplifting. There isn't a happy ending," I tried to explain.

"I'm fine with that," Char said. "Actually, I'd prefer that. I'd rather cry than be cheered up. I'm sick of conflict. Sick of drama."

"I agree," Bobby added. "There are times I love a sad movie where I can sit in the dark and cry."

"Share your story with us," Mike begged. "We need to – and, I especially need to – escape for a while."

"Then put lunch on the table, and I'll tell you about my friend Jim."

We took our seats and began to pass the food around the table family style. Once everyone had been served, and the compliments given, Karen looked at me and nodded.

I began by telling them about my friend and former design client, Jeff, who introduced me to Jim, and how Jeff had been the arts and entertainment editor for the local Hillmont paper for many years. He had contacted my author's website for an interview when *Nathaniel & the Midnight Movers* was released. I knew what I was getting into, but Jeff was clueless. He assumed the author on the book's cover was who he'd be meeting. He didn't know that person was a ghostwriter and the actual author was me, his friend of many years.

"He must have been shocked when you showed up," Karen said.

"I bet most people are in shock meeting Ricky," Val added with a devilish grin.

"He was confused at first, but I explained that since many of the stories in the book were based on former clients, I didn't want my name to be attached."

"Did he believe your book was fiction?" Peggy asked.

"At first," I replied. "But somewhere along the way, he caught on. Much later he explained that it was the way my eyes would light up talking about it."

"I can see that," Mike said sweetly.

"May I stop you for a second and ask what we're all dying to know?" Gayle began. "Is your book fiction or nonfiction?"

I hesitated, although I had expected someone would ask me that question. Last night I had decided that it didn't really matter anymore. Either they would accept me, warts and all, or not.

"It's a true story," I admitted. "I am Nathaniel."

There was a moment of silence and then laughter. Karen pulled out a ten-dollar bill from her pocket and handed it to Val.

"We had a bet going, and Karen just lost," Val said, gloating.

"And I take it you've known all along," Peggy said to Mike.

"Yes, well, I knew bits and pieces," Mike admitted.

"Then Dean *was* in your gang? One of the Midnight Movers?" Karen asked.

"My uncle Dean?" Maggie added.

"Yes," I said, adding, "He was the least involved member and was included more by necessity than by greed."

"If my baby brother were here today, I'd whoop his ass," Peggy said.

"I'm sorry," I apologized. "It's like the book says. I started it, then Greg joined in. Then Dean, our third roommate. When he moved back in with us, so much didn't make sense to him. He realized that there was no way we could afford everything we had."

"But you never stole from an individual, right? Only furnished models. Things from stores?" Char asked.

"Except that one time," I admitted. "The antiques."

"And this is where the story gets crazy. I had design clients who were originally from Hillmont," Mike shared. "They purchased a condominium, had their furnishings delivered, but had yet to move in. Then one night, someone cleaned them out. At that point, they decided to go ahead and move to Bellwood to be near their kids. They had lost so much, including an antique lowboy."

"We did not clean them out. But yes, we did take quite a bit. Dean told that story to his wife, June," I added. "She remembered he specifically mentioned an antique lowboy and gold mirror."

Maggie looked at Karen with concern. Karen smiled and said: "Actually, June and I are quite close. She's been a dear friend over the years."

"After Dean died, June shared that tale with me, not realizing the significance," Mike explained. "I suspected that it was true and, in turn, I confronted Ricky – at the wedding of Dean's daughter, no less. Later, Ricky showed me his manuscript and a Polaroid of the lowboy."

"We were also at the wedding that weekend," Bobby added. "Karen, Peggy and me. You never said a thing."

"Just like Gator knew he could confide in Mike, I felt I could trust him as well," I said.

"Okay, back to Jim," Maggie instructed, trying to get my story back on track.

I told everyone that Jeff had reviewed Jim's book before Dylan came forward, and the truth started slipping out. Jeff realized that Jim and I were kindred spirits. Because of Jim's peeping, he had been able to stop Dylan's predator from molesting him. And, if that story was true, then most likely other stories in Jim's book were true.

Conversation stopped as everyone pondered what I had just told them.

"Let's stop for dessert," Karen suggested, breaking the silence. "Anyone want coffee?"

"Yes, please," Mike said. "And then Ricky can tell you about the rest of this adopted family of misfits in Hillmont."

"Kind of like us?" Gayle asked.

"More than you know," I said.

CHAPTER

Once dessert and coffee had been served, everyone settled in for more of my story.

"I've got to say that I'm still having a hard time understanding why Connie was out joyriding with Ming," Char began. "And why they would drive by here."

"If it was intentional – and how could it not be – they wouldn't have known that we would be outside to see them," Val added.

"Connie didn't even try to hide," Bobby reminded us. "It was like she wanted to be seen. And yet, she didn't wave or acknowledge us like any friend would have."

"Do you think they knew we were here?" Karen asked. "Or

were they riding by each of our homes out of curiosity?"

"I feel like we're being stalked," Peggy added. "I don't like it."

"I would think Ming would only be interested in Mike's clients' homes," I added. "Gayle and Karen."

"I'm ready for Connie to come clean and tell us what the hell is going on," Gayle said. "This is not like her at all."

"And I want to stop thinking about it and let Ricky continue telling us about Jim," Mike said in a frustrated tone.

"We'll get to the bottom of this," I assured him. "Now, where was I?"

I explained that quite a bit happened once Jim's book was published. The most important thing was Dylan and Jim connecting. Dylan had first learned about Jim's book from my friend, Jeff, who frequented the restaurant where Dylan works.

"The social worker, who had helped Dylan in his younger days, let him know that his abuser had moved back to town and lived close to Jim and Matt," I explained.

"Matt was the therapist boyfriend?" Maggie asked to clarify.

"Yes," I replied. "And at that point, still a good guy. Or at least that's what everyone thought."

I revealed more, including Dylan's plan to put signs in his abuser's yard to let his neighbors know of the pedophile's past. Jim wanted to help, and even Matt agreed.

Dylan talked with Jeff to see if the paper might cover the incident. So, Jeff learned Jim's book was a true story. Regardless, he wanted to help.

"Jeff brought the two of you together?" Peggy asked. "Two authors with books of fiction that were, in fact, memoirs. Right?"

"Right," I confirmed.

"You see," I began, even though I knew tears would fall, "Jeff's son had been molested by a family member. They didn't learn about it until their son took his own life."

"Oh, my God," Gayle said in shock. "I can't even imagine the pain."

"Jeff offered to interview the abuser after the signs were posted under the pretense of letting him have his say," I explained. "But instead, Jeff found him dead when he arrived."

That wasn't entirely true, but for now, I thought that was all that needed to be said. I shared how this brought everyone together.

"There is so much more to tell, and I don't want to bore you," I said.

"I don't think anyone is bored," Char spoke for the group.

Continuing my recap, I shared that we learned later that Matt's kidnapping was staged. When Jim helped "rescue" Matt, it caused Matt to improvise by putting the blame on his wife *and* her brother.

"But how did Jim find out the kidnapping was fake?" Peggy asked.

"When Jim began his sessions with Matt, he encountered Diana, an agent with the State Bureau of Investigations. She was working undercover for Matt's wife. Jim was using an alias to keep Matt from discovering who he was at the time. And, of course, Matt had his own secret life going on as well," I explained. "By the time everything had come to light, Jim and Diana felt a connection and became close friends."

"Basically, everyone had a secret?" Karen asked.

"Jim wouldn't let it go," I replied. "He felt Matt was cheating on him. With Dylan, of all people. Eventually, he went to see Matt's previous paramour, his wife's brother

Chris, in prison. Chris thought Jim had figured it out, but Jim was completely surprised."

I added that Chris revealed the kidnapping had been staged. In the original plan or at least the plan Chris knew, all of the blame was to be put on his sister, Matt's wife, Julie. Jim wouldn't rest until he knew everything. He finally went to see Julie in prison under the pretext that he wanted to write a book about her.

"She was hesitant to talk with him, but then she came around, and it blew his mind," I said excitedly. "That's when Jim put the pieces together and realized in Dylan's younger days of hustling to make ends meet, he had not only met Matt but had become Matt's obsession."

"Dylan, the boy Jim rescued, had been involved with Matt – who was now Jim's lover?" Maggie asked in disbelief.

"What the?... Val stammered."

"Yes, and Dylan was underage when he was first involved with Matt," I continued. "Matt had treated Dylan like a possession. Finally, he knocked on Julie's door asking for help."

"How did Dylan know where she lived?" Gayle asked.

"Matt was brazen enough to take Dylan to his home when Julie was out of town," I answered. "Julie didn't believe Dylan at first. But she said he knew things that he shouldn't have known. Eventually, she realized he was telling the truth and that he was afraid of Matt – something Julie had lived with in the past."

"What did she do?" Bobby asked. "Did she help him?"

"Yes, she helped Dylan get free of Matt," I affirmed. "But when Dylan met Jim years later, it caused him to be reconnected with Matt. Neither said anything because Matt and Dylan both had a lot to lose."

"After Jim finally learned about the Julie and Dylan connection, he took Dylan to see her in prison. He said that seeing the two of them together, almost like a mother and child reuniting, brought him to tears. Julie was so proud of the man Dylan had become and excited that he had been promoted to sous-chef at work. Jim knew he wanted to write about it – a second book that wouldn't be billed as fiction. He wanted to tell their story – set the record straight. He felt it might be an atonement for his past deeds."

"But that didn't happen," Karen acknowledged.

"No," I replied, getting choked up. "He had started writing and even talked with his agent and editor. They stood by him but encouraged him to be honest about his first book."

"If you don't want to talk about it, Ricky, it's okay," Karen voiced. "I'm sure we all would understand your need to stop at this point of the story."

"I had mentioned earlier our friend, Roberta Ann, who does estate sales. When Matt went to prison, she bought his condo next door to Jim. And get this – it turned out that she and Diana are first cousins," I explained. "The rest of us that night were at Diana's waiting for them to show up."

Mike, with a look of concern, took my hand. I smiled to assure him I was okay.

"A while back, I decided to write down the events of the night of Jim's death and what transpired later. A remembrance for me as well as an explanation for others. I needed to stop thinking about it – obsessing about it. But I also didn't want to forget. I asked Mike to make copies. If you'd like to read what I wrote, I promise we can discuss it once you're done."

Mike had brought a manilla envelope with him that no one had seemed to notice. He got up, crossed the room, and brought it to the table. He treated it as if it were a sacred document, gently handing a copy to each of them. Like an accident on the side of a road, I couldn't look away. I needed to see my friends' reactions as they read – needed to know that they got it – that they now understood.

My friend and fellow author, James "Jim" Norris died in April of 2020 after being violently attacked in his home. The family, as we called ourselves, had planned to have dinner at Diana's apartment that evening. Jim and Roberta Ann were carpooling since they lived next door to each other. Dylan and his new boyfriend, Trevor, would be there. And my other half, Mike, had made the three-hour drive from Bellwood to go with me.

Dylan, Trevor, Mike and I had made ourselves comfortable in Diana's sitting room. We were enjoying a glass of wine and making small talk while waiting for Jim and RA to arrive. Jim was rarely late. And RA, always needing to beat the early-bird shoppers at her Trash & Treasures estate sales, was never late.

Dylan and Trevor had worked together at Tattinger's Restaurant for the past three years. Because of Jim's nudging and encouragement, Dylan finally opened up to Trevor about his past. For the first time, they had shared a bed the previous night. There was still an afterglow on their young-in-love faces.

"I'm getting concerned," Diana said when her call to Jim went straight to voicemail.

"RA's did the same," I added after leaving her a message to call.

"Something's wrong," Diana voiced. Her years working for the State Bureau of Investigations made me take her concern seriously.

"Why don't Mike and I go check on them?" I offered, motioning for Mike to stand.

"I'm going," Diana announced. "You guys stay and enjoy dinner."

"Hell, no," Dylan snapped as he and Trevor put down their glasses, ready to leave.

"Put a note on the door and turn off the oven," I suggested. "We're all going."

The five of us piled into Diana's sedan and held on for dear life. When we pulled into Jim and Roberta Ann's condominium complex, blue lights were flashing, and a barricade kept us at bay. Diana parked and told us to wait. With her badge in hand and a look on her face that dared anyone to stop her, she charged forward.

As the four of us waited, it began to sink in that something was terribly wrong. I remember getting out of the car and seeing Diana comforting Roberta Ann in the distance. I felt such relief, but only for a second, because I knew, we all knew, that whatever had happened – it had happened to Jim.

"It's Jim," Diana said without emotion when she returned to the car. "He's gone."

Dylan let out a heart-wrenching cry.

Diana was trying to keep her emotions in check. "Take the car back to my house. You're welcome to wait, but I know it's going to be a while. Try to eat something. I'll call when I can, but for now, I'm still learning what happened."

"Diana?" Dylan pleaded.

"Take care of each other," she said and then walked away.

What we eventually learned was Roberta Ann had walked over to ride with him and became concerned when Jim didn't answer his door. At first, she thought he might have forgotten she was going with him and had left without her. But still, that didn't explain why he didn't answer his phone when she called. Calling once more, she heard his phone ringing from inside. She tried the doorknob, but it was locked. Roberta Ann went back home, got the ladder out of her garage, and leaned it against the eight-foot-high brick privacy wall separating their courtyards. She then climbed the ladder and looked over. It had taken her a few moments to realize what she saw through Jim's window. Then, when everything came into focus, she called 911.

—•—

One week after Labor Day in 2020, the weather was still as sweltering hot as mid-July. I was sitting in the comfort of my cool apartment, staring at my laptop. I had opened a group email from Diana. Her message said to click on the provided link with the assurance that it would explain everything. She revealed that she planned to add it to Jim's author website eventually. And yet, I couldn't bring myself to follow the simple instructions. Diana, who had been MIA since Jim's funeral, was also requesting by email, a "family" dinner that weekend.

I had not seen much of anyone over the past months. Of course, Mike still visited me in Hillmont, or I'd spend time with him in Bellwood. Roberta Ann and I had talked several times, both of us expressing our concern about Dylan's state of mind. Our friend Jeff, who had become Dylan's benefactor, succumbed to cancer last December. And now Jim, who had prevented a pedophile from molesting a seven-year-old Dylan fifteen years earlier, had been murdered. The back-to-back deaths had taken their toll on Dylan, who was already fragile. I'd kept in touch with Trevor, who was now living with Dylan, and was relieved that he was looking out for him. But I had not seen or talked with Diana other than a few brief words following Jim's funeral. When she would respond to one of my texts, it was usually a day or two later with as few words as possible.

Jim had surprised Diana when he left his estate in her capable hands – news we learned when she made Jim's funeral arrangements. Another surprise was that he would be buried next to Jeff and Jeff's son. Jim, having no family of his own, had been the executor of Jeff's estate and accepted Jeff's offer to be buried with his family. After Jim's graveside service Diana revealed, without explanation, that she would be taking a leave of absence from the Bureau where she had been an agent for many years.

As the video opened, Diana was facing the camera in a simple sleeveless black dress, with her brown hair, longer than when I last saw her, pulled back in a ponytail. At forty-two years old, with just a hint of makeup, she could still pass for someone in their mid-twenties – advantageous for the numerous undercover cases she had worked during her time at the Bureau. With no idea of what she was about to say, I braced myself and clicked "play."

"My name is Diana," she began, "but if you're familiar with the James Norris novel, PEEPER, then you may know me better as the character, Donna Green."

She took a deep breath.

"Jim Norris was my friend," she continued. "No, let me start over. Jim Norris was my best friend. That's not easy for me to say because I'm not the type of woman who has best friends. I'm a little bit too in your face – often too sarcastic. I have no problem speaking my mind, and my sense of humor can be a tad dark."

I sat there mesmerized but also confused as to where she was headed.

"The thing is, Jim and I were alike in so many ways. He could give as good as he could take. Often infuriating, selfish and needy, he could then turn around and be kind, sympathetic, and generous. I'd catch myself wanting to strangle him, and other times, wanting to comfort him and tell him everything would be alright. There are very few people whose opinion matters to me, but Jim's did."

What are you trying to say, Diana?

"My best friend was brutally murdered – stabbed over and over and over again by some goddamn closeted homophobic piece of shit, and I couldn't save him. I was with the Bureau, an agent for the

fucking Bureau of Investigations – I should have known. I should have protected him. I should have..." She paused, then added in a whisper, "I should have saved him."

As tears began streaming down her cheeks, I wanted to reach through the screen and let her know that it wasn't her fault. None of us knew.

"I'm sorry," she said after composing herself. "I didn't mean for that to happen."

She hesitated for a moment longer before continuing.

"Jim surprised me by leaving his estate in my hands," she explained. "However, there were instructions, responsibilities, thoughts and ideas without a plan on how to make it happen. Again, infuriating but generous."

After clearing her throat, she revealed, "I took a leave of absence from the Bureau. I loved my job and never thought I'd want to leave. But here we are – what's it called? Social distancing? The Bureau and I are taking a break so that I can do what my friend, my best friend, Jim, has asked of me."

"Jim had begun the follow-up to his first book, PEEPER. In fact, he was more than halfway through and had notes of things he still wanted to include. Along with professional help, I have completed

that book for him. He was so excited about it. One, because of what he had learned – the truths revealed. And two, because he wasn't going to pretend it was fiction. He felt the stories were too important to lie to you, his readers."

"Uh-oh," I said. "What are you doing, Diana?"

"People speculated that Jim's first book, PEEPER, wasn't fiction, and they were correct. He had promoted it as such, but then, as one tale after another was revealed to be true, Jim struggled as he tried to keep his stories straight. He was embarrassed by his peeping Tom past – afraid that would be the only thing people would see in him. I'm not ashamed to admit that I had already made up my mind about the person he was before I got to know him."

I knew Jim would be smiling at Diana's confession.

"The thing is, with this new book, Jim was prepared to admit all of that – to come clean. The plan had been for him to tell the truth during his scheduled appearance on the Tonight Show. But, as we all know now, he never had the chance. His new book, REDEMPTION, tries to answer the things Jim questioned – the things that all of us have questioned. As the pieces fell into place, Jim learned his characters' actions were just reactions to the things life had dealt *them – things we couldn't see. And just as Jim had been judged by you and me, there was so much more to their story."*

"Jim saw this second book as an atonement for the harm he felt he had imposed on others. Real or imagined."

"There's a second book?" Bobby asked. "Is it out?"

"Yes, there is a second book, but it hasn't been released yet," I explained. "Diana has promised us advance copies any day now. Spring is the preferred time for new releases. So it will be released in April. One year after Jim's murder."

"What you wrote," Gayle began, "breaks my heart. It is so personal, intimate, and conveys the love for your friend."

"You really are an excellent writer, Ricky," Karen added. "You should be doing a second book, too."

"Mike, you received the email and link that Ricky talked about?" Peggy asked.

"I did," Mike answered softly. "It was... was one of the most emotional things I had ever watched."

"You were right to chastise me," Val admitted. "I was a shit for saying what I did. I didn't know Jim. And like Diana said, I was quick to judge him without knowing his whole story. Please forgive me, Ricky."

"There is nothing to forgive," I said. "You're not alone in thinking that. But to those of us who knew him, it hurts. Hopefully, this new book will change some minds."

"Diana is amazing," Char said. "I hope to meet her one day."

"Thank you for sharing this – *sharing him* with us," Karen said sincerely.

I looked over at Peggy, who was wiping a tear from her eye. Maggie had taken her hand, brought it to her lips, and kissed it.

"So much death," Peggy said. "So much pain. But so much love for those special to us."

"I can't imagine losing one of you," Bobby began. "Much less, losing two of you in just a few short months of each other."

"Let me ask you this," Karen began. "Could Diana help with the Ming trouble?"

"I don't mind asking her," I replied, "But I would think an attorney would be the first route to take."

"Then what about the attorney from Jim's book?" Maggie asked. "Glitter-Gate."

"Oh, God, I had forgotten that part," Bobby exclaimed.

"Matt's wife threw pink paint and glitter on him."

"That's a good idea," Mike said, turning to me, "Would you mind asking him?"

"Not at all, but I honestly think I should tell Diana what's going on," I replied. "I'd like her take on everything."

"Okay, here's a crazy idea," Karen excitedly announced. "What about inviting Diana to come to Bellwood?"

"For that matter, what about Dylan and Trevor?" Val asked. "And Roberta Ann?"

"I'd love to meet them all," Maggie added.

"Diana and Roberta Ann could stay with me," offered Karen.

"And Dylan and Trevor could stay with us," added Mike.

"What about this weekend?" Peggy asked.

"Slow down, guys," I said, holding up my hand. "This is a little sudden."

"Look," Peggy began, "We all want to meet them. Diana can give you guidance about Ming. And Dylan could give us pointers about the piano bar. You know, especially if we're turning it into a restaurant."

"That's an excellent idea," Mike added.

"Dylan and Trevor are off Sundays and Mondays when

Tattinger's is closed," I explained. "Maybe they could drive over on Sunday and stay the night."

"Perfect," Maggie shouted. "Charlie's will be open Sunday night, and then we'll have Monday to pick their brains."

"All I can do is ask," I relented, thinking to myself, *God help us.*

CHAPTER

Seven

"You want me to do what?" Diana asked as if she was shocked by my request to come to Bellwood.

"You heard me," I replied. "You know you want to."

"And you would be wrong," she stated. "What did you have in mind? Did you think we'd sit around, braid each other's hair, and talk about boys? Then maybe a rousing chorus of Kumbaya? Thanks, but no thanks."

"Don't be such a bitch!"

Silence on the other end of the phone.

"Diana?" I asked. "Are you still there? I'm sorry."

"I'm here," she said in a much softer tone. "You sounded so much like Jim that I had to catch my breath. You're right. I am. And sometimes I need to be reminded."

"You, Roberta Ann, Dylan and Trevor," I continued.

"I doubt that RA will come," Diana said.

"She's already agreed to," I responded.

"You asked her first?" she snapped. "I assume you've already asked Dylan and Trevor?"

"I have, and they thought it sounded like fun," I replied, knowing I had ticked her off.

"Why am I the last one asked?" she questioned in a pissed-off tone.

"Because you're the biggest pain in the ass," I answered, feeling cocky since we were talking by phone and not in person.

"Say what?"

"Seriously," I began, "I didn't want to get you on board and then find out the others couldn't join us. I think too much of you to waste your time."

"Good save, as well as a smart move," she relented. "So, what's on the agenda?"

"Our friends want to meet you," I explained. "They've read Jim's book, and mine as well. They're anxious to get to know you."

"Sort of like a fan club?" Diana kidded.

"These are Mike's longtime close friends. They're good people, and I think you'll enjoy meeting them," I explained.

"Ricky, I don't mind meeting them, but I'm not in the market for new friends," she said.

"What's that supposed to mean?" I asked, taken back by her comment.

"I don't want to get close to anyone new and then have them taken away in a blink of an eye. Jim and Jeff broke my heart. And, yes, I have one. I just can't go through that again."

"I understand. And, if truth be told, I feel the same," I admitted. "But come visit, and we'll have fun. I promise."

"There's something you haven't told me," Diana said. "Right?"

"How did you...?"

"Years of experience," she replied. "Spill."

"We need your advice. Mike had a business associate. The relationship ended badly, and now she's out for blood," I confessed. "And it appears that she might be stalking him, actually, all of us. Everyone is concerned."

"Stalking?" Diana said, snapping to attention. "Not on my watch."

I shared what had happened so far and how it appeared to be escalating. She said, as I had expected, that trying to sabotage Mike's business would be best handled by an attorney. Basically a cease-and-desist letter of sorts. But the drive-by the other day had her concerned. I knew she was thinking of Jim and still blamed herself for not protecting him. I didn't want our request to be something to bring her pain.

"What's this skank's name?" she asked in her professional voice.

"Ming Leatherwood."

"Ming?" Diana questioned. "Are you shittin' me?"

"I shit you not," I replied with attitude.

"That can't be real," she said. "Is it?"

"No," I admitted and then told her the name Mike had shared with me.

"That's more like it," she said with satisfaction. "And the husband?"

"Gator."

"Gator?" Diana questioned. "Like that song about a gator getting your granny?"

"Are you talking about 'Polk Salad Annie' from the late 1960s?" I asked in shock.

"That's it," Diana replied. "Tony Joe White."

"How could you possibly know that? You weren't even born yet!"

"Research for a case a few years ago," Diana answered smugly. "So we've got a backwoods bayou thing for the husband and a Chinese dynasty thing for the wife – fake names attached to an English surname."

"That about sums it up," I said.

"Just what was his given name?" Diana asked.

"That I don't know, and neither does Mike," I admitted. "We had thought there would have been an obituary or memorial service that could give us more information. But so far, we're not aware of anything. However, I do have their address, and maybe you can find out from the property deed."

"I'll look into it," Diana offered. "Do you have a photo of her?"

"I know there's one on Mike's website of the two of them at a trade show," I replied.

"Hold on. I've pulled up his website. Let me scroll through the photos," she said. "What am I looking for?"

"Dyed dark hair and animal prints," I replied.

"Got it," Diana said a moment later. "Not unattractive, but she should be issued a fashion citation for that outfit. It looks like something I'd wear when I'd go undercover as a hooker. How old is she?"

"Same age as Mike and me," I answered, laughing. "Oh, and don't be fooled by the picture. Mike calls her the queen of photoshop. He said she wouldn't let him post a pic until she had the chance to freshen it up – smooth out the rough edges."

"That's why she looks closer to fifty?" Diana asked. "So, we add vain to her profile?"

"Definitely. Since you're on leave from the Bureau, are you going to be able to find out much?" I asked.

"I still have friends and connections here *and* in Bellwood. So don't you fret, Prissy Pilferer," she confirmed.

"Prissy Pilferer?" I repeated, trying to not to laugh.

"I thought it was time you had a nickname, too," she said, giggling.

"Oh, so you don't like Nathaniel?" I asked.

"That's your professional cat burglar name," Diana explained. "Prissy Pilferer will be my term of endearment for you."

"Well, ain't I special?"

"Okay, I'll get the gang together, head out Sunday morning, and get there in time for lunch," she said. "Will that work?"

"Perfect," I replied. "Just come on to Mike's, and then you can follow Karen to her house. The girls with Karen and the boys with Mike and me."

"Whatever you say, P.P."

"I think I prefer Prissy," I responded to a dial tone.

—•—

We let everyone know that our friends would be coming Sunday and should arrive around lunchtime at Mike's home. In our quest to make it easier on everyone, Mike decided to ask one of the local restaurants to provide the meal. Our plan was to hang out at home that afternoon and then go to Charlie's in the evening. As far as Monday, it would depend on when they needed to get back on the road.

Karen was first to respond, saying that she'd be happy to do brunch Monday at her home. Bobby and Maggie followed with they'd bring a dish to help. Val offered as well, with Peggy coming in next to last. It appeared that, like our luncheon a few days earlier, everyone was willing to whip up or pick up whatever was needed.

—•—

Mike had a couple of appointments on Friday and one installation to take care of. He assured all three clients that he wasn't going anywhere, and again, he suggested Ming wasn't thinking straight because of grief. To those outside of our group, Mike came off as concerned and wanting to be supportive of Ming's loss – giving her the benefit of the doubt. But I knew he was hurt, furious and struggling to hold his tongue. Going after a grieving widow, no matter how evil she appeared to be, was not a good look.

That evening we had dinner out – just the two of us. Then, around eight, we stopped by Charlie's for a drink. At that hour, on a Friday night before COVID, all the booths would have been taken, and we'd be bumping into couples on a crowded dance floor. But tonight, I counted twenty-seven patrons, one bartender (when normally there would have been two or three) and Maggie. Peggy was pleased to see us and said she was looking forward to Sunday.

"I'm anxious to meet your friends," she confided to me. "And curious to see if Dylan might have some ideas for our new venture."

"And I want to meet Diana," Maggie said as she walked over. "I think we're about the same age."

"You are," I confirmed. "So we'll have the boys in their twenties, you, Diana and Roberta Ann in your forties, and the rest of us in the sixty range."

"And me," Peggy added. "Older than dirt."

"By the way, we usually call Roberta Ann by her initials," I explained. "RA."

"RA, GG, TLC," Maggie commented. "Anyone else who goes by initials?"

"Well," I began as Mike looked my way, "Diana just nicknamed me the Prissy Pilferer or PP."

"Love it," Mike said. "Don't you?"

I gave him my best resting bitch face, which caused the three of them to burst out laughing.

"What's so funny?" Bobby asked, walking toward us. He

and Karen had slipped in unnoticed.

"I didn't see you come in," Peggy remarked, sarcastically adding, "You know, with all the crowd and such."

"Don't worry. There will be standing room only once Charlie's Piano Bar opens," I said. "Piano Lounge? Cocktail Lounge or Bar?"

"Let's just go with Charlie's for now," Peggy said.

"Speaking of which," Mike began, "will you shut down during renovation?"

"I think that we'll have to, don't you?" Maggie replied. "But, if everything could be timed in a way that one thing followed another with no holdups, do you think it could be done in maybe no more than a week to ten days?"

"Anything's possible," I replied, trying to sound optimistic as Mike shook his head from side to side.

"I want to close, so we can have a grand reopening," Peggy added. "We're really not making any money now, so we won't be losing all that much."

"Speaking of which," Bobby said, "Do you have a budget in mind?"

Mike and I were both curious and relieved when Peggy said

she had a nest egg. But, she also needed to have an estimate because it might have to be done in phases. We assured her that we weren't charging anything and would try to find the most bang for the buck.

"I appreciate that, but I'm not expecting free," Peggy said, adding: "Cheap, yes – free, no."

We promised that, after this weekend, we'd pull together some ideas with estimates of expenses. In my mind, our priorities were to fend off Ming, try to win Connie back, and then the makeover of Charlie's.

CHAPTER
Eight

On Saturday, I helped Mike get the house in order for our guests. There wasn't that much to do but he did want fresh linens on the beds, the bathroom sparkling, and our lunch order placed with one of the nicer non-chain restaurants in town. We were up early Sunday morning making sure that we had thought of everything. Mike was anxious since this was the first time any of them had seen his home. I tried to reassure him that it was perfect – elegant and inviting. Somewhat formal and yet comfortable. I also reminded him of Diana's apartment, which was perfectly fine, but not ready for *Architectural Digest*. And, Dylan hadn't really made many changes to the home he inherited from Jeff. It still had that after-divorce-starting-over feel, even though I had chosen some of Jeff's pieces.

"Are you already here?" I asked when my phone rang and Diana's number appeared.

"Yes, we're in Bellwood, and RA has the GPS going with some demanding bitch barking out directions," Diana said in a gruff manner.

At that point, I realized how much I had missed her, as well as the others, when I heard laughing in the background.

"You're much earlier than I expected," I stated.

"Are we interrupting some mattress merriment?" Diana asked in a sexy voice.

"Heavens no," I replied a bit too quickly after seeing the look on Mike's face. "I mean, we're done. It's safe to come over."

Mike saw Bobby's car, then Peggy's, followed by Karen, pulling into the drive like a funeral procession or parade. He opened the door and stepped out to greet them. I walked over, still holding the phone, and saw that Maggie had ridden with Peggy, and Gayle was with Karen.

"The others just got here, so come on. Your adoring fans await your arrival," I said, joking into the phone.

"Please keep the paparazzi at bay," Diana instructed. "This GPS skank just told me to turn, and I missed it. Now she's recalculating. We'll be there eventually." And then, in typical Diana fashion, she hung up without saying goodbye.

"They're almost here," I announced. "Earlier than I expected."

"What about the food?" Karen asked.

"It's scheduled for a twelve-thirty delivery. So I guess any minute now," Mike replied.

"I'm nervous," Maggie admitted. "I want them to like us."

"How could they not?" I asked. "They're the ones who should be nervous."

"You're a good man, Ricky Hunt," Peggy said with a wink.

A catering van from the restaurant was next to arrive. Two adorable young men got out, opened the van's door and began gathering covered dishes to bring in. Bobby took one look and quickly offered to help.

"You think he's looking for a boyfriend?" Karen asked.

"Tell me that you'd turn either one of them down," Peggy said to Karen. "Hell, I'd take sloppy seconds."

"The line forms behind me," Gayle added, surprising all of us.

"What a bunch of horny old broads," Val commented as Bobby came in with his arms full. "And that includes you, Sugar Daddy Bob."

The eye candy in the kitchen turned to look at us old geezers as we broke out laughing.

"Sorry," I said, apologizing for our behavior.

The blond god with perfect skin recognized Peggy. "You own Charlie's, right? It's so retro – like stepping back in time."

"It's about to get a makeover," Maggie said defensively, "into a piano bar and restaurant."

"Cool," remarked the dark-haired boy wonder as they went to fetch more from their van. "We'll have to check it out."

"How soon will the makeover be done?" Bobby asked. "You don't want to keep those two waiting."

"Careful gramps, your pacemaker might get overly stimulated," Val added, causing us to once again laugh hysterically.

"What the hell is so funny?" Diana snapped, standing in

the doorway. "I was expecting rose petals along the sidewalk with balloons and confetti."

"Let me just say that I love her already," Val announced.

"You might want to wait until you've spent some time with her," Roberta Ann remarked. "I'm RA, by the way."

You could definitely see the family similarities when RA and Diana were standing side by side. Roberta Ann looked slightly older and was a few pounds heavier.

"Come here, you," I demanded, wrapping my arms around her. I then turned to Diana and opened my arms wide as she just stood there. "You know you want some of this."

"I go back and forth on whether to hug you or arrest you," Diana retorted.

Mike had his arms around Dylan and Trevor and began the introductions. I noticed Bobby's eyes were open wide, taking it all in.

The two catering boys had finished unloading. I gave them a credit card for the order and a hefty tip in cash. Maggie commented how they, one blond and one with dark hair, were almost the mirror image of Dylan with his blond locks and Trevor with his dark hair and smoldering eyes.

Caterer Blondie asked Dylan and Trevor about joining them tonight at the new dance bar. Dylan thanked them but said they already had plans with friends at Charlie's. To which Blondie replied that they might see them later.

"Dylan and Trevor just got to town, and they're already drumming up business for the bar," Peggy said with a smile. She then opened her arms and motioned for Dylan to come to her. He did, and she wrapped them around him and said: "God bless you for everything you've been through in your life. I'm sure none of us knows the half of it. I'm sorry I didn't meet your friends Jeff and Jim, but I've already been told how much they loved you."

Then nodding to Trevor to join them, she told him to take care of Dylan and protect him. She then told Dylan to do the same.

"You two hold onto each other and never let anyone or anything come between you." She then kissed each one on the cheek and gave them another squeeze before letting go.

Diana looked at me and smiled before turning to hide her tears.

"And, let me just say," Roberta Ann began, " that I love *her* already."

"Wow," Mike whispered. "Come on in. Bathrooms are down the hall and guys, you can choose either room to put your things in. Please make yourself at home. Wander around, relax and just chill. I'm going to put the food on the table."

"I'll help," Char offered, with Val tagging along behind her.

"My heart feels so full right now," Val shared.

"Mine, too," Gayle added, joining us in the kitchen. "The Connie I know would have loved this. She should have been here."

"We'll get her back," Mike said, trying to comfort her. "But for now, we need to gather as much information as possible to figure out how we can make that happen."

Mike's three bedrooms are off the same hallway like most typical 1960s ranch-style houses. The two guest rooms are on the front, with Mike's bedroom on the back. Dylan and Trevor chose the bedroom farthest from where we slept, allowing us all maximum privacy. They brought their overnight bags in, and I gave them a moment to freshen up.

"Give us the tour," Diana demanded. "Let's see if Mike's any good at this interior design crap."

"She's not always like this," RA said to everyone. "Usually, she's worse."

"It's okay," Val commented from the next room. "They're used to me, so nothing will shock them."

"Is Diana getting surly?" Dylan asked, rejoining us. "We're always cautious about taking her out in public."

"You do realize that I'm standing right here?" Diana growled.

"Maybe a good lunch will help," Bobby suggested. "And then a nap."

"Come on, sweetie," I instructed. "Let's fix you a plate."

Once we were seated and the food passed, Diana asked if anyone had questions.

Although she acknowledged that the Bellwood folks probably know more about the Hillmont folks because of the books.

"Maybe we should be the ones asking questions," RA suggested. "Like, what do all of you do for work – past and present? How are you connected?"

"I'll start," Bobby offered. "I grew up in Bellwood, but being so much younger than these guys, I didn't meet everyone until I was in my twenties."

"Younger?" Mike asked. "By two years."

"Anyway, I worked at Blooming Idiot Florist as a designer. I met Mike, who was working in the same strip center at Furniture World, fell in love, and moved in together. Of course, Mike was still in love with Dean, but we made it work. Eventually, Mike and I bought out the owner of the flower shop, and I ran it. Later, Karen bought out Mike, and she and I kept it going until we sold it a little over a year ago."

"Interesting," Diana commented.

"I'll go next," Karen began. "Dean and I dated in college, and when I moved back here, he followed. We married, but my best friend, TLC, came between us. Mike and Bobby knew but never told me. When I found out, I walked away from my marriage and my friends. It was years later before I reconnected with Mike and Bobby at Dean's memorial service."

"TLC?" Roberta Ann asked.

"Tammy Lynn Cunt," I whispered, then laughed at the surprised look on her face.

"I'm sorry," Trevor said, "but who is Dean?"

"Thank you," added RA. "I'm so confused."

Bobby, Karen, Peggy, Maggie and Ricky all began to speak at once until Diana put up her hand, motioning to stop. She pointed at Karen, who said, "My first husband."

"My childhood best friend and lover," Mike admitted.

"My college roommate and a reluctant midnight mover," I added.

Diana pointed to Maggie, who answered: "My uncle."

And then finally to Peggy, "My baby brother."

"Shit!" Dylan whispered.

Gayle raised her hand, and Diana nodded to her. "My high school boyfriend."

"Damn," RA muttered. "Who isn't connected to Dean?"

Diana looked over at Char and Val. "He was our friend," Val said sincerely.

"So, you're missing Dean from your family, and we're missing Jim and Jeff from ours," Diana stated.

She then raised her glass of ice tea in a toast. "To friends we've lost."

Turning to Karen, she asked. "Were you done?"

"Just one more thing. Before working with Bobby, I worked at Suzy Q's women's apparel in the mall, which is how I met Gayle and Connie."

"Okay, next," Diana said, pointing to Gayle.

"I went to school with Mike, Gayle and Dean. Met Karen through the store and reconnected with everyone at Dean's memorial."

"I didn't work," Peggy announced. "I was happily married until I wasn't. The bastard cheated on me. I moved back to Bellwood to look after my parents. Charlie, our beloved friend, saw the unhappiness in my life, pretended to be in a bind and asked for my help at the bar – known as Sugar's – just for the weekend. I never left, and I met these wonderful friends. I had a purpose. I was needed. My parents accepted it, knowing it was where Dean had felt at home with his friends. My evil sister did not approve, and we parted ways. Good riddance."

"And?" Diana asked, knowing there was more.

"And then Charlie got sick. He tried to hide it until he couldn't. I kept the bar going when he wasn't able. Eventually, we lost him. That son-of-a-bitch had owned the bar all along and left it to me. *To me!* He knew I needed it, and he knew I'd keep it going. I changed the name from Sugar's to Charlie's, and now I'm hanging on as long as I can."

"So your family actually lost two as well. Dean *and* Charlie. We're two for two. No more losses," Diana said. "Promise me. No. More. Losses." Then, turning to Maggie, she nodded.

"I'm the newest 'family' member. My mother is Peggy's evil sister, Alice. She disowned Peggy and now me, for admitting that I'm a lesbian. Peggy has taken me in and like Charlie did for her, has given me purpose. I want to make her proud and turn Charlie's back into the thriving business that it once was."

"Let's take a break," Mike said.

"Does anyone need anything?" I asked.

"I'd almost forgotten about Connie," Gayle said. "Do you think they know we're together? Maybe driven past your house?"

"I don't know," Mike replied. "I don't want to spend any more time looking over my shoulder."

Diana walked toward me and pulled me aside – away from Mike.

"I don't want to like them. I don't want to be their friend," she began. "I just want to help."

"I know," I said to reassure her.

"But I already do. You were right. They're amazing," she added, causing me to smile.

"Thank you," I replied.

"Wipe that smile off of your face," she snapped. "I can't understand why Mike would leave Bobby for you. He's adorable."

"Bitch!"

"That's more like it," Diana said with satisfaction.

"Why don't we sit in the den?" Mike suggested when everyone came back together. "Or the porch, if it's not too cool."

"I vote for the porch," RA said, and Karen agreed with her.

Once we were seated with our refreshed drinks, I asked: "So who's the alpha in your family? I assume that you've guessed ours." Diana blew me a kiss.

All eyes turned toward Peggy.

"Was that alpha or simply the oldest?" Peggy said, laughing. "Fine, Ricky, you start."

"I met Dean in college, as well as Karen," I began. "I met Mike when I came to town to be in Dean and Karen's wedding. I reconnected with Mike years later at Dean's daughter's wedding, as well as Bobby, Karen and Peggy. RA and I met when I hired her to do my estate sale. And I met Diana after everything went down with Matt, his wife and brother-in-law. Jeff and his wife hired me long ago for design work, but they separated after the death of their son. And, as I told you the other day at lunch, Jeff reviewed my book, introduced me to Jim, which led to knowing Dylan and then finally Trevor."

"RA?" Peggy asked.

"As Ricky said, we met when he hired me. I knew he was trouble then, but he was so much fun. I met Jim when his next-door neighbor was moving and hired me for the sale. And as you know, 'D' and I are first cousins. Through them, I met Jeff, God love him, and Dylan. Through Dylan, I was introduced to this sweetie, Trevor."

"And you're the one who found Jim on that night?" Peggy said as time stood still.

"Yes, I did," RA said softly.

I shook my head slowly from side to side as Maggie placed her hand on her aunt's arm – both of us signaling Peggy to stop.

"I'm sorry," Peggy said. "That was insensitive."

"It's okay," RA said sweetly. "I'm grateful I was the one who found him – a friend who loved him – and not some stranger."

"I'll go next," Trevor offered, taking the attention off of RA and receiving a whispered thank you in return.

"Okay young man," Peggy said.

"I grew up in Hillmont, going through the public school system and then junior college," Trevor began. "My first and only job has been at Tattinger's, one of the nicest restaurants in town. Jeff came in often and would ask for me. I'd always read his column so that I could talk with him about it. When I mentioned his review of a peeping Tom book to Dylan, I had no idea of the connection. I'd had a crush on Dylan from the start. And, although he was always nice and polite, it was clear that he wasn't interested in me."

"Not true," Dylan added.

"Okay, he wasn't ready for a relationship. I didn't know why until I read his story in Jim's book," Trevor explained. "I met Ricky, Jim, Diana and RA when they came to the restaurant for Valentine's Day and asked for my table. Jim played matchmaker, convinced Dylan to take a chance on me, and I'm so grateful that he did."

"Dylan, are you ready?" Peggy asked sweetly.

"Yes, ma'am," Dylan replied. "My story is an open book, literally. You know about my childhood – the rescue. Reading Jim's book – my story – then being able to meet him and thank him was incredible. But Jim did so much more for me. You know, I've always thought that I didn't fit in. That my background would make people uncomfortable. But Jim showed me that we were kindred spirits deserving of love. And Jeff, dear Jeff, took me into his home and then left his house to me when he died. I don't know if I would have ever had a home of my own. Or the opportunity to share a home with someone I love."

Maggie asked. "I understand you've trained for and been promoted to the position of sous-chef?"

"Yes, I've been very fortunate," Dylan replied. "I hope to have my own restaurant one day."

I saw Maggie look at Peggy and immediately knew what they were thinking.

"I think you will," Peggy said. "I believe in you."

"Now, alpha to alpha, what's your story?" Peggy asked Diana.

"I think you know," Diana replied, playing it coy. "Law enforcement, always on the straight and narrow path until that bastard James Norris entered my life. Such an infuriating man. Oh God, how I miss him. Through him, I met Ricky and Mike, Dylan and Trevor and Jeff. Now, Jeff was a saint. Of course, there have been numerous, even more unsavory, characters connected to these guys as well."

"And you have Jim's second book ready. His book *Redemption*?" Peggy asked. "You did that for him?"

"And for me," Diana admitted. "I needed to make my own amends."

"Ricky shared what you said in your video to them. You feel guilty for Jim's death – although there wasn't anything you could have done short of moving in with him as a bodyguard. As I understand it, the murderer was a high school friend who probably wouldn't have rung any alarm bells."

"Still..." Diana said, beginning to get emotional.

"Still," Peggy repeated. "You need to forgive yourself. I had to do that with Charlie. As much as I tried to protect him, I just couldn't. I blamed myself for the longest time."

"Peggy," Val said, only to have Peggy wave her away.

"I know, and you know," Peggy said directly to Diana. "It was meant to be. We don't know why and we may never understand. I couldn't save Charlie or Dean any more than you could save Jim or Jeff. But we can carry on their memory and do good in their name."

It was one of those rare times that Diana was silent. No smart-ass remark or comeback. She knew, and we all knew, that Peggy was right. We needed to go on with our lives because none of them would want anything less for us.

CHAPTER
Nine

"Are you ready to talk about your friend Connie and this Ming chick?" Diana asked, changing the subject.

"I am," Mike answered eagerly.

"Somebody fill me in about Connie," Diana began.

"She's one of my best friends and has been since elementary school," Gayle began. "We lost touch during our college years and right after we got married. But we reconnected when we both had our first child. And, we have remained tight ever since."

"She's sweet, thoughtful and gentle," Mike added. "And she's pretty much the opposite of Ming."

"So why are they hanging out now?" Diana asked. "What common thread could there be?"

"Politics, for one," I offered. "They both were happier with the previous President. And, not at all with the one before him or the one we have now."

"I will never understand that, especially being in law enforcement. Crime after crime has been committed by that previous President, bragged about and then repeated. And still, no formal charges, so far," Diana said. "Sorry for the rant. But it's a bigger mystery to me why any woman would vote for and stand by him."

"Before anyone outs me," Gayle began, "I did vote for him. I believed the promises told in the beginning and thought we needed a change. Sadly, they were just lies. But I'm going to go out on a limb and say that I think there are problems on both sides of the aisle."

"I believe we can all agree that our system is broken and that there is plenty of blame to go around," Mike said.

"Okay, we've got politics," Diana repeated.

"I don't think Connie is as far gone as Ming," I added. "After all, she did get the vaccine, and I've seen her wear a mask."

"And Ming is an anti-vaxxer?" Diana asked. "I assume her husband was as well."

"Yes," Mike confirmed.

"Then I don't think politics would be the only thing binding them," Diana stated. "I don't know Connie, but if she believes in being vaccinated and wearing a mask to protect herself and others, then wouldn't she be upset at Ming for exposing you and not telling you that she did?"

"I believe Connie would have had a problem with that for sure," Gayle said.

"Then what else?" Diana asked.

"We think they may have connected over online games," Val added. "They both play them. But, we don't know how they would have originally figured that out."

"As far as I know, the only time they met was when I worked with Connie for a second time recently, and Ming made draperies for one of her rooms," Mike said.

Gayle offered, "That means they could have been playing for a couple of years or more."

Diana asked, "Is that a strong enough connection for Connie to be fine with Ming coming after Mike's business?"

"We wondered if maybe Ming told Connie that Mike had agreed to give it to her, and she believed her," Char added.

"Wouldn't Connie have said something or asked Mike about it?" I questioned.

"Let's put Connie aside for now," Diana suggested. "What do we know about Ming?"

Mike began to share all he could think of, since he had known her the longest. They had worked together for nearly twenty years. At first, it was just a few jobs here and there. But then he used her more and said the quality of her work kept improving. He also said that early on she'd have a different installer on each job because no one could please her. Eventually, Gator left his job, whatever that was, and worked with Ming installing and delivering her finished products.

"It helped when Gator took over the installations," Mike explained. "You know, just having the same dependable person each time."

"Did she work exclusively for you?" Diana asked Mike.

"No. I didn't have enough jobs at the start to keep her busy," Mike explained. "She has worked with several designers, and I would imagine a few jobs on her own. She even worked for Val's mom at one time."

"That was long ago and didn't end well," Val shared. "Two strong personalities, but only one could be boss. When she left, some things disappeared. She denied it and it got tense. My mom wrote it off, told no one, and was done with her."

"Were you ever aware of her stealing?" Diana asked Mike.

"No, never even thought about it. No one ever complained about something missing."

"She wasn't married when she worked with my mom," Val added. "Maybe Gator kept her in line."

Diana asked Mike if he could think of any reason she'd turn on him and try a hostile takeover of his business. He said no and was baffled by her actions. He shared that the last contact was a text where he had expressed concern and asked if she or Gator had COVID. Also, he asked if they had been vaccinated. Mike showed us the text on his phone to prove his point.

"I knew the answer, but I wanted confirmation," Mike told Diana. "I never got it from her. Eventually, I learned Gator had gone into the ICU."

"For a normal person, that wouldn't be a reason to make them want to destroy you and your business," Diana explained. "But she may not be normal. Gator's death may have unleashed something in her. She might feel guilty for not getting vaccinated. She might not want to admit it was her fault and therefore needs to blame someone else."

Mike said that's what he initially thought. He had decided that if she needed him to be her punching bag, then he'd take the lumps and bruises.

"What about the drive-by the other day?" Diana asked. "Is there any way that Connie or Ming would have known you had gathered at Karen's?"

Everyone said no. It had been a spur-of-the-moment decision.

"Who last talked with Connie?" Diana asked.

"I guess that's me," Gayle admitted.

"I'm not doubting you, but are you sure you didn't mention anything about the luncheon or even going over to Karen's?" Diana asked.

"Trust me, I thought long and hard about our conversation, and no, nothing came up other than me asking what the hell was going on and Connie telling me lies that Ming supposedly said," Gayle explained.

"Another possibility could be that Ming was following one

of you, and you led her there. Finding all of you was just an unexpected bonus," Diana explained.

"I'm the most likely suspect," Mike admitted. "It's my business that she wants."

"True," Diana agreed. "But that's not always the case. She could be jealous of Karen or Gayle. She might think one of them flirted with Gator. Maybe she's secretly in love with Bobby. Or maybe she hates lesbians. She could have any one of a dozen off-the-wall reasons to follow any of you. And, then by sheer luck, she found the whole gang."

"That doesn't make me feel any better," Karen admitted.

"Connie said she didn't want to come by Charlie's," Gayle began, "because she was uncomfortable in a gay bar."

"I'm confused," Diana stated. "Hasn't Connie been your friend for years? And she knows you're gay? And she has been comfortable going in Charlie's in the past?"

"Yes," Mike answered.

"But she has a problem now?" Diana asked. "Does Ming have an issue with gays?"

"I never thought so," Mike responded. "It was never a

problem between us. Plus, in her line of work, she'd encounter gays in every aspect."

"I think her opinion has changed," Bobby began. "I'm looking at her page right now, and there are two new posts. One about gay schoolteachers grooming students."

"Grooming, as in the pedophile sense?" Char asked.

"It appears so," Bobby confirmed. "And another post about the so-called 'Gay Agenda' of the Democrats – through television, movies and books. Some of the comments her friends have posted are frightening. The milder ones want gays fired and the extreme ones think we should be rounded up and put in a concentration camp."

"That's hate speech," Diana said. "I don't understand why these social media sites don't take shit like that down."

"That post alone has over 200 likes," Bobby continued. "Her friends list is now up to 340 followers."

"It's growing by the hour," I said. "I don't understand how that can happen so fast."

"I'm looking at it now," Val added. "The posts have multiple shares. These idiots share it to their page and then their minions share it to their page and on and on."

"So, Ming's hate speech is gaining traction?" Peggy asked.

"It appears so," Bobby replied. "I don't see where she has mentioned Mike yet."

"If she does," Diana explained, "it will make you a target."

"As far as Maggie and me," Peggy added. "we haven't met Ming. I'm not aware of her ever coming into Charlie's."

"That's good. Still, I want all of you to be mindful of your surroundings. Look around when you're going to your car. When you're driving, check to see if anything looks suspicious," Diana instructed. "You said she drove a conspicuous van, but does she have a car, too?"

"They had a silver Toyota sedan of some sort," Mike offered. "I don't know."

"The perfect car to blend in and not be noticed," Diana said. "Regardless, be on the lookout. It doesn't appear that she wants confrontation, but you need to be cautious. Call someone if you see her. Park in a crowded area with people around. And if you notice her near your home, call the police."

"Do you think we're in danger?" Peggy asked.

"I always think the worse and try to prepare for it," Diana answered. "Don't open the door unless you know who is on the other side and you feel safe. I told Jim that, but his killer was an old friend from high school, and he wasn't concerned. If you have outside cameras, use them."

"We believe that Jim didn't use his, or he would have seen his classmate holding a knife," I added.

"Even if it's Connie at your door, be sure she's not a Trojan horse leading the way for Ming," Diana said. "Listen, I don't know either of these women. I'm just going on my years of experience. It could all be a misunderstanding that will blow over. Or there could be a totally different agenda in the works. I just want you to be careful."

Diana went on to explain that she'd be calling in a few favors from people she knows in this bureau office, as well as checking out Ming's past. She said she had already decided she needed to stay a bit longer, but that the others could go back tomorrow. She asked me if I'd give her a ride back to Hillmont when I go.

"Of course," I said. "You can borrow my car while you're here."

"Thanks, but I think I'll rent a nondescript sedan to tool around in," Diana replied.

"Why don't we pack up some of the leftovers to send with you to Karen's," Mike offered. "It's already four-thirty, and I know Peggy and Maggie need to get ready for work. I thought whoever wants to go to Charlie's tonight could join us around seven. Does that sound good?"

Everyone agreed. Gayle said it gave her enough time to feed her hubby and that she'd pick up Karen and Bobby on the way.

"I'm happy to pick you up too," she offered to Val and Char.

"Thanks, but you know I like having my wheels in case I want to scoot out early," Val explained.

"Then it's settled," I pronounced. "Charlie's at seven."

After the girls left, Dylan asked if it would be okay if he and Trevor just rode around for a bit. Mike offered to show them the sites, but they wanted to explore on their own. He gave them his key fob, and they promised not to be gone long.

"Did you pick up on Maggie and Peggy thinking they could get Dylan to move here to open the restaurant for them?" I asked Mike once the boys had gone.

"Not at all," he said. "But that would be perfect for them."

"Which them?" I asked.

"Definitely Peggy and Maggie," he began. "Maybe not

so bad for the boys either. A fresh start. With the sale of Jeff's house, they could easily find something affordable to buy here."

"But could Peggy pay a competitive and fair wage?" I wondered. "And what about Trevor? I'm sure he has aspirations of being more than a waiter – not that there's anything wrong with that."

"I know that you'd miss them," Mike continued. "So you might just have to move here as well."

"If I ever do move to Bellwood, it won't be for Dylan and Trevor," I admitted.

"What would be your motivation?" Mike innocently asked.

"Why don't you see if you can motivate me right now? We've got the house to ourselves," I said with my best devilish grin.

—●—

Dylan and Trevor returned around six in time to shower and change for a night at Charlie's.

"I don't know how to tell you this," Dylan began. "We saw the Ming's Fabrications van."

"Saw it? Where?" Mike asked with visible panic across his face. "Parked or on the road?"

"Or following you?" I asked.

"I think she was following us," Trevor added.

"How would she know to follow you?" Mike asked, not catching on.

I explained the obvious. "Because they were driving your car."

"I drove, and Trevor helped with directions. We were both looking around at everything when he mentioned a van had been behind us for several blocks," Dylan explained. "I made a couple of turns, and it stayed with us. When I pulled into a parking lot, it drove past us."

"That's when I saw the Ming's Fabrications signage," Trevor said. "There was only the driver – an older woman with dark hair."

"That's her," Mike confirmed. "At least Connie wasn't with her."

"Do you know when she first got behind you?" I asked. "I'm wondering if she was near the house waiting."

"There is only one way out of the subdivision. She could have been waiting near the entrance," Mike explained. "If she had been there very long, she would have seen Val's truck and

Bobby, Karen and Diana's vehicles."

"But, she doesn't know Diana or what she drives," I reminded him.

"I imagine she is trying to figure out who we are," Dylan added. "And why we had your car."

I said I'd call Diana and let her know it was clearly Mike being stalked.

Diana called me before I had the chance.

"Connie called Gayle, and Gayle called me," Diana began without a hello. "Gayle said Connie made small talk and apologized for being MIA. Then she said she missed everyone and wondered if Gayle had seen Mike recently."

"What did Gayle say?" I asked, now with her on speaker.

"Gayle mentioned seeing you at Charlie's the other night, and then she got ballsy and added that she saw you for lunch at Karen's house. She reminded Connie that she already knew that since she and Ming drove by the house."

"You go, Gayle!" I said before I thought. "What was Connie's response?"

"She ignored the comment by going back to her mission to find out about Mike," Diana explained. "Connie told Gayle that she had heard Mike had company, young guys, and she wondered if he was cheating on Ricky."

"She knows better," Mike said in a huff.

"What was Gayle's explanation?" I asked, dying to know.

"Get this – she said she didn't know, but maybe the two of you had rented a couple of escorts."

"She didn't?" I screamed as Dylan and Trevor laughed so loud I couldn't hear. Mike looked like he was about to pass out.

"How does she already know about the boys?" Diana asked.

"I was getting ready to call you," I replied.

I told her about Dylan and Trevor borrowing Mike's car and then realizing a van was following them. They said Connie wasn't with her. I added that she must have been near the neighborhood's entrance and, therefore would have seen all of them leaving.

"The plot thickens," Diana said. "So we now know it's Mike that she's after. That makes it easier to keep a lookout. I'm sure she's wondering why you guys are getting together so much. She appears narcissistic enough to think it's all about her."

"Isn't it all about her?" I asked.

"At this point, it's about keeping all of you safe."

CHAPTER

Ten

Mike and I were the first to arrive at Charlie's. I had already explained to the boys that it needed of a facelift, and I told them about Peggy's idea to turn it into a piano bar.

"The outside is kind of drab," Dylan commented as we approached the front door.

"So is the inside," I added. "But Mike and I are going to come up with a makeover plan."

"And Peggy has already found a baby grand," Mike added.

Maggie and Peggy rushed over, taking the boys by the arm to guide them on a tour of the bar. Dylan must have spotted the photos of Mike and me in the grouping displayed behind plexiglass on the wall since he turned and laughed.

"I still think it might be a good idea," Mike began, "But I hope Peggy doesn't come on too strong and chase them away."

"Peggy? Too strong?" I repeated, laughing.

Val and Char entered and waved to Dylan and Trevor before joining us. Maggie had once again created a makeshift banquet table where we could gather. The other booths were filled, and several couples were on the dance floor, which I took as a good sign. Bobby, Karen and Gayle arrived, waved, and then headed to the bar to get drinks. We joined them before taking a seat at what had become our "signature" table.

"I imagine there are lots of interesting stories that could be told about this place," Trevor commented. "It's homey and inviting – very old school with the jukebox and tiny dance floor."

"But the kitchen is hopeless," Dylan added. "Way too small for actual food service if you're serious about a restaurant. You're going to have to consider bumping out a wall."

"What about an open kitchen concept?" Val suggested. "That way, you could have a larger kitchen but with it being open, it might not make the bar feel smaller."

"That could work," Dylan acknowledged. "Except the noise might interfere with the piano player."

"You're right," Val agreed. "I didn't think of that."

"Since you're leaving tomorrow," Mike said to Dylan, "can we take a serious look at the kitchen right now, and you can give me some idea of how much room would be needed."

Dylan, Mike, and Peggy headed toward the back as Roberta Ann and Diana entered.

"Let's get you something to drink," Maggie offered, steering them toward the bar.

"I'm still freaked out about Ming following the guys. Of course, she thought it was Mike," Karen said as Diana and RA joined us.

"I'm glad we now know that it's Mike she's after. I'll plan on tailing him tomorrow and see if I can spot her," Diana explained.

"Anyone else bothered that Connie called for the sole purpose of finding out who was driving Mike's car?" Gayle asked.

"Yes, but your escort line was priceless," Trevor said.

"Did she sound like she was alone?" Diana asked. "Or was she possibly with Ming?"

"I don't know," Gayle replied.

"Okay, did she sound like herself? A casual conversation with a purpose? Or did it seem like she was being coached or had a script to follow?" Diana asked again.

"I think a script," Gayle answered. "She wasn't going to veer from her mission."

"At that point, neither Ming nor Connie knew you guys were in town," I pointed out. "Two young men driving Mike's car was unexpected, but she wouldn't know if it had anything to do with her."

"If she is the narcissist that I think she is, then everything is about her," Diana explained. "When you go out tomorrow, drive Ricky's car. I just wish there was another way in and out of your neighborhood. I'll come over and scout out the entrance on the way."

"She knows my car, too," I explained. "She's been by the house when I've been in town."

Mike and Peggy returned to the table.

"Where's Dylan?" I asked.

"He's still looking around," Peggy explained. "His wheels are turning. He's thinking about a functional kitchen, where everything would go, and how much room is needed to make it fit."

"I think we'll need to come out about ten feet," Mike added. "It doesn't appear to be a load-bearing wall. But we'll probably lose that last booth."

"Then you're keeping the booths?" Bobby asked.

"I don't know," Peggy answered. "It depends on what they come up with and how much it's going to cost. I do have some savings put back. But again, I can't become destitute in my old age."

"I think you should give her a quote as if money weren't a problem," Diana said to Mike and me. "Then a quote for the next step down and another for one after that."

"Thank you. I'll get right on it," I replied sarcastically.

"I'm serious," Diana insisted. "It may be in her budget or, if not, it might be possible to get the money another way."

"Like one of those online fundraisers," Trevor suggested.

"Or Ricky could have another estate sale," RA joked. "The last one raked in the bucks, big time."

"I'm sure it was quite profitable, considering what he paid for everything," Val added with a wink.

"And I'm sure I don't know what you're talking about," I replied demurely.

Dylan rejoined us, saying he had some ideas and would sketch them out to discuss with us in the morning.

"I wish you guys didn't have to leave so soon," Maggie whined.

"Wow, that was pitiful," Char remarked. "Does that usually work?"

"It's been known to," Maggie replied, giggling.

A couple of guys rushed in and yelled: "Anyone in here drive a black Wagoneer?"

"I do," Mike hollered back as he jumped up and walked toward them.

"There's an old woman with shoulders like a linebacker scratching something into the paint."

Mike went running out the door with Diana right behind him. I followed but told everyone else to stay put. Ming had already fled. However, carved into the side of the black paint was "Liar."

Diana instructed Mike to call the police and file a report. She went back inside to ask the guys who witnessed the incident for a description. They described Ming perfectly – right down to the animal print jacket.

"That was ballsy," Bobby said. "With your car parked in front, she had to know someone would see her."

"Again, narcissist," Diana reminded us. "She has a sense of self-importance, yet she plays the victim. Females can be just as vindictive as males – jealous and competitive. And usually more manipulative, which might explain Connie and the mirror guy Danny, helping her."

"Surely she knows that she might get caught," RA commented. "Or would she think that by blaming someone else, she'd get away with it?"

"I think the latter," Diana replied.

About ten minutes later, Mike came back in and said the police had shown up almost immediately. "The smirking cop said that he thought it was probably a jealous boyfriend. I think because I'm parked in front of a gay bar that it wasn't worth his time."

"Damn, I should have waited with you," Diana said in full defender mode. "I would have wiped that smirk off his face."

"I would have loved to have seen that," Val remarked.

"The one smart thing Ming did was not carve something like "faggot" or "queer" because that could take it into a hate crime," Diana explained.

"But liar?" Dylan questioned. "She thinks you're a liar because you didn't tell her about her husband's blow job?"

"I guess," Mike replied. "Or liar because of her delusions that I'd give her my business."

"She's in her own world right now," Diana said. "with her posts and followers dangerously heading into conspiracy theories – possibly QAnon. She may have other voices playing in her head."

Karen brought up Connie again and her concern for her. From what Diana was saying about Ming, she feared Connie could be in trouble. But none of us knew how to get Connie alone and talk some sense into her.

"Oh, wait!" Gayle exclaimed. "Tuesday at ten."

"What's Tuesday at ten?" Karen asked.

"Connie has a standing manicure appointment," Gayle explained. "She has had it for years. Never misses."

"Unless Ming causes her to miss it," Char added.

Gayle said. "I've got to try."

"Then I'm going with you," Diana insisted. "I can wait outside until you're sure Connie is alone. Of course, if Ming drives her van, it would be easy to spot in the parking lot."

"Would you be able to talk with Connie freely?" Bobby asked.

"He has a point," Peggy said. "With the manicurist and other customers around."

"What if you wrote her a note? Suggesting a place where you could meet," RA suggested. "Some place that's special to the two of you."

"I could try, but who knows if she would even show up? Or if she could break free from Ming," Gayle replied.

"Do we think she's spending every free minute with Ming?" Val asked. "Surely, someone would think that strange. Her daughter, maybe?"

"She's married, isn't she?" Dylan asked. "She has to go home eventually, or her husband would be suspicious. Right?"

"Can't you just go over to her house?" Maggie asked. "Do you think she wouldn't let you in?"

"I don't know," Gayle replied truthfully. "She's got one

of those cameras at her front door, so once she sees it's me, she might not answer. What if Ming is keeping tabs on her?"

"Bobby, can you whip up a flower arrangement for first thing in the morning?" Trevor asked.

"Sure," he replied. "I'd need to run to the grocery store and get flowers since I don't have the shop anymore. Why?"

"What if I delivered a bouquet to Connie in the morning?" Trevor offered. "It could have a note from you with a place to meet. Or, I could say you're in your car down the street and want to see her."

"If she sees that face in her security camera, she'll throw caution to the wind and fling the front door open wide," Dylan said with a wink.

"It's hard to argue with that," Bobby commented lustfully.

"I say give it a try," Diana added. "Gayle, she may have been wanting to talk to you but can't. I like the note idea. Let Connie write a reply with a time and place. We don't know her schedule or what Ming might have planned for her."

"I hope it works," Peggy remarked. "I just feel there is an explanation for why she's acting this way."

"Playing Devil's advocate – if Connie wanted to talk with Gayle, then why doesn't she call her?" Val asked. "It's not like she and Ming are together every minute of every day."

"To continue that thought," Char began, "even if Ming checked Connie's phone to see who she talks to, couldn't she use her husband's phone or her daughter's?"

"She's got a point," Karen added.

"That's all true," Diana said, stating the obvious. "My first thought is fear. If Connie talks to one of you and we intercede in some way, then *if* Ming is holding something over her, she'd be afraid it may come out. Or maybe she's too embarrassed about her behavior."

"If she's not, she should be," Peggy added.

"Then why do we think she'll talk with Gayle now?" Maggie asked.

"Honestly, I don't know she will," Gayle replied. "But I do know that Connie is in some kind of trouble, and Ming appears to be volatile. I'd never forgive myself if I didn't try everything possible to help."

"So, we're going to do this?" Bobby asked.

"Yes," Peggy and Gayle said in unison.

"What about Danny?" Diana asked. "I know he doesn't live here, but he might have something to share."

"Do you want me to call him?" Mike asked. "I doubt that he'd come clean by phone."

"Break up with him," RA suggested. "Tell him that you no longer wish to work with him and that you need for him to pick up his mirrors."

"Wouldn't that make him mad?" Dylan asked.

"Yes, but he may want to try and make it right," RA responded. "And throw Ming under the bus."

"That's my cuz," Diana said proudly.

"I'll do it in the morning," Mike agreed. "I no longer trust him and just want to be done."

"Let him know that you're aware of Ming's email and his involvement," Karen suggested. "We don't know to what extent, but he won't realize that. He will probably start scrambling for an excuse."

"The one advantage of Ming's attack on my car is that I'll need a rental, too," Mike said. "It might take her a while to figure out what I'm driving."

"Put your car in the garage until your insurance company

is notified and you get an appointment with a body shop," I instructed. "I'll take you and Diana to a rental agency in the morning."

"Do you think the cops will make an effort to track her down?" Mike asked Diana.

"We might need to help them," she replied. "I'll see if there are any exterior cameras in the area that caught her in action. We know who did it, but we still need evidence for an arrest."

"I know Charlie's isn't your top priority," Peggy began, "but, if I'm being honest here, the bar is drowning. I can't keep pouring money into it until I have none left. I have faith that Maggie's idea will work. When I go, I'd like to be able to leave it to her, knowing that I didn't fail Charlie."

"You're not going anywhere, and please don't worry about leaving anything to me," Maggie stressed to her aunt.

"We'll get Dylan's feedback on the kitchen ideas in the morning and work on a plan right away," Mike said. "I could use a diversion."

"Thank you," Peggy replied sincerely. "Anything I can do to take down Ming and rescue Connie, I'm ready and willing."

The crowd had thinned out since tomorrow was a working day for most of the patrons. We talked for a while longer and even danced to a few songs before saying good-night. Dylan remarked that most of the music on the jukebox was older than him. However, Trevor thought the selection was fabulous with its mixture of standards, show tunes, and country.

"Trevor loves Broadway, although he's never been," Dylan informed us. "He has vinyl, CDs and even subscribes to an online Broadway station that he plays in the car."

"I never knew this about you," RA said. "Next time one of the traveling Broadway shows comes to town, I'm taking you."

Trevor's eyes lit up as he gave Roberta Ann a hug.

"Do you sing?" Karen asked. "Because when the piano bar is up and going, you'll need to join in."

"He's got a great voice," Dylan answered, bragging on his beau.

I watched Maggie look at Peggy again, and I could swear I saw a lightbulb turn on above her head – probably thinking Trevor would be an asset for whoever gets the pianist job.

"Okay, you two, we need to go," I announced. "We have a full day tomorrow with the mystery flower delivery, discussing the makeover, getting rental cars, and whatever else comes up before you head back home."

We said our goodbyes to Peggy and Maggie, stepped outside, and were quickly reminded of the damage to Mike's car under the streetlight. Diana spotted a camera at the business next door and said she'd check tomorrow to see if it captured Ming in action. Then, Karen rode back with Diana and RA, and Gayle dropped off Bobby. Val and Char left in Char's Caddy from their days of working at the dealership.

I told everyone to keep a look out for Ming's van and to call if they spotted it. However, two blocks down, I saw the van in an empty parking lot with the motor running.

"What do I do?" Mike asked hurriedly.

"Just keep going," I instructed. "We don't want a confrontation tonight."

Out of spite, Mike waved to her as we passed. Ming put the van in drive, and we assumed she would follow us. Instead, she turned in the opposite direction.

CHAPTER
Eleven

Bobby arrived at the house at eight the next morning with a stunning floral arrangement.

"You found those flowers at the grocery store?" Mike asked.

"Actually, I stopped at two different stores. I bought loose flowers at one and a bouquet at the other," he explained. "I tore the bouquet apart, tossed out the carnations, and then put it back together again. I added the Alstroemeria stems from the other store and snipped a few twigs of greenery from my yard. I wish I had more options."

"Are you kidding?" I asked. "It's stunning. The combination of those flowers held by Trevor will be too beautiful for Connie to resist."

"Thank you," Trevor said, blushing. "What about the card?"

"I brought one with me, but you're going to have to tell me what to write on it," Bobby said.

We decided on *To Connie, with love, your friend Gayle. Please tell me when and where we can meet and give the card back to the delivery man.*

"I don't get a name?" Trevor asked.

"The less Connie knows, the better," I replied. "We still don't know if she'll be willing to talk or immediately report back to Ming. To keep you safe, you're just the delivery guy."

"Got it," Trevor acknowledged.

At that moment, Diana walked through the front door without knocking.

"Keep the damn door locked," she yelled.

"And good morning to you, too," I said sweetly.

"Yeah, good morning. Seriously, you need to be more careful. I can't go through another..." she paused, then said: "Just be careful."

I knew that Jim was on her mind and his carelessness. She was right. We couldn't take chances.

"Sorry," Mike said. "You're right."

"Are we all set?" Diana asked. "Trevor, you take my car

since no one knows it. Dylan, you and Bobby follow in Bobby's car. You know where you're going, so you don't have to stay close to him. Maybe circle Connie's house to make sure you don't see Ming."

"I can't imagine she'd be staking out Connie's place this early in the morning," I said.

"We don't know shit," Diana reminded me bluntly. "So we take any precautions necessary."

"What about us?" Mike asked.

"Ricky's going to drive us to the rental car dealer. That way, we both can have a car, and yours can stay in the garage," she explained. "Trevor and Dylan have my number, and they better call at the first sign of trouble. Mike, you know where Connie lives, right? So, you could get us there immediately if anything goes awry."

"Are you expecting trouble?" Trevor asked.

"No, but again, let's be careful," she repeated. "And stay alert, just in case Ming is lurking and itching to follow someone. We don't want her to see us go anywhere near Connie. Got it?"

Trevor decided to follow Bobby's car to Connie's street. Bobby and Dylan turned so as not to be spotted. Diana had them on speaker phone, keeping us updated. Bobby reported that he didn't see any signs of Ming's van but would continue to circle the block to make sure.

Mike and Diana rode with me to pick up their rental vehicles. We were about to pull into the lot when Bobby called and said Trevor had made the delivery and was leaving the area. We parked and waited to hear the outcome.

"She seemed surprised at receiving the flowers," Trevor began after meeting up with Bobby and Dylan. "I told her that I had been asked to wait until she read the card in case she wanted to send a reply."

"And did she?" Diana asked, anxious for the answer.

"I offered her my pen to write something down, but she waved it away," Trevor continued. "She said to tell Gayle that she will call when she is able and until then to please leave her alone."

"That could mean a couple of things," I commented. "One, that she's afraid of Ming finding out."

"And two," Diana butted in, "that she isn't ready to talk. I'm not sure there is anything else that we can do to convince her."

"Do you want me to call Gayle and fill her in?" Bobby asked. "In fact, I can let the rest of them know."

"Thank you," Diana answered, surprising me since she is usually all business and forgetful of common niceties.

"And, in case you haven't had a chance to check," Bobby added, "Ming has a new post. It's congratulating those who didn't give in to the hysteria, were never tested, never complied, and knew COVID was bullshit from the start."

"But she and Gator *were* tested," Mike said, raising his voice. "It's in one of the texts Ming sent Victoria. And they believed in science enough to get the antibodies shot."

"If COVID is bullshit, then what does she think was the cause of Gator's death?" I asked.

"One last thing," Bobby continued. "Her friend base is now at 665."

Mike let out a long sigh, then regained his composure and asked Trevor:

"Did she at least tip you?"

"Hell, no," Trevor replied. "And, I gave her my best smile!"

"Why don't you go back to the house and wait," Diana suggested. "This shouldn't take long."

After we hung up, Diana admitted that she had thought it had zero chance of working, but at least we tried. She also said that she didn't feel Connie was acting as Ming's accomplice – but that there *was* something making her participate.

The leasing agent was all teeth and tattoos and enthusiastic to the point of making me think he was on something. He told Diana that he had the perfect car for her – a cherry red Mustang. Fortunately, Diana showed restraint and informed him that she'd prefer to blend in rather than stand out. He came up with a white Nissan sedan.

Mike told Mr. Hyper that he didn't need anything fancy or sporty – just reliable. You could see the look of disappointment on the man's face. But he had another Nissan sedan in a shade of gray that fit the bill.

Then we drove back to Mike's home to meet up with the boys.

"Did Bobby already leave?" Mike asked Dylan when we returned.

"He said something about going over to Connie's and asking for his flower arrangement back," Trevor replied. "How she didn't deserve his creation."

"Surely he was kidding," Diana said.

"Yes," answered Dylan smiling. "Although he was pissed about it."

"What time are you guys heading out?" I asked.

"Probably no later than three," Dylan replied. "I'd like to get home before dark."

"If you're ready, why don't you give us your ideas for the bar's kitchen?" Mike suggested.

"I've got to use the ladies' room, and then I'll run by the Bellwood office and see if anyone can give me the scoop on this thing called Ming," Diana announced.

Mike's phone rang, and we heard him say: "This is he." Followed by "What did you just say?" And then, "No way in hell," in a raised tone.

We all stopped to listen, curious about what was upsetting Mike.

"You've got that all wrong," Mike said strongly. "She's lying to you, and if you print any of that after I've told you differently, then I will sue you and the paper. Got it?"

After disconnecting, he said: "Damn, I miss phones where you could slam the receiver down to end the call."

"What was that?" I asked.

"Someone from the Living section of the local paper is writing a story on how I've passed the torch to my close associate Ming Leatherwood."

"You've got to be kidding," Diana added.

"She wanted a couple of quotes for the article that will run in the Sunday paper, with sneak peeks online starting Thursday," Mike explained.

"What if they hadn't called you?" I asked. "The article would have been like an official announcement that you're retiring and Ming's now the boss."

"It makes you wonder what else she might be planning," commented Dylan.

"You need to call GG and tell him what's going on," Diana instructed. "I'm dialing his office now."

Once connected, Diana said who she was and that she needed to speak to George right now.

"Yes, I'll hold," she replied and then whispered to us, "but not for long."

Mike and I looked at each other and then at Dylan. We were surprised that Diana not only had Mr. Glitter-Gate attorney on speed dial but that she had enough clout for him to drop whatever he was doing to take her call.

"Good, and you?" She said. "Now, let me tell you what's going on, and then you're going to tell me what you're going to do about it."

Diana reminded GG – aka Glitter Gate, aka George Grant – who we were and our connection to Jim and Jeff. She explained the situation in a no-nonsense way and then handed the phone to Mike.

"Now, I've really got to pee," she announced and charged down the hallway.

Mike walked into the dining room and sat at the table to talk. Dylan, Trevor and I gave him some privacy and moved into the den. I sat in the club chair next to the fireplace, and the boys shared the sofa after moving the tapestry pillows out of the way.

"Do you think she can be stopped?" Dylan asked.

"Legally, yes," I replied. "What worries me is what she'll do before she's stopped."

"I'm going to check that outside camera by the bar to see if we have enough to press charges," Diana explained when she rejoined us, taking the matching chair opposite me. "That is, once I get my phone back and can leave."

"I didn't know you were so chummy with GG," I commented.

"Working on Jim's estate," she replied, thinking that was enough.

"And, how's that coming? Is everything settled?" I asked.

"No, and it may never be," she replied. "The book deal and the new book deal, along with the possibility of some kind of movie will keep it going for some time – generating income that needs to be invested."

"What about the new book?" Dylan asked. "I know you say you've finished it, but since I'm a part of the story, I'd like to know what was said."

"Don't worry. I didn't write it. That's not one of my talents," she began. "His agent had someone who could finish what Jim started. Since I knew the story and all of the players, I stood over his shoulders to make sure everything was as close to Jim's voice as possible."

"I'm sure the writer enjoyed that," I remarked with my best sarcastic tone.

"Not so much," Diana responded with a laugh. "But, I

wasn't going to let anyone screw it up. You'll be pleased."

"But you never talked with me about it," Dylan continued. "You didn't interview me. Didn't you have questions?"

"Dylan, I didn't talk with anyone. Jim had already written more than half of the book. And he had a rough draft of the final chapters. These are Jim's words – his account of what happened. It's from his perspective," Diana explained. "I chose not to discuss it with anyone for fear of changing what Jim had intended. You know as well as I do, Jim would not have written anything that he didn't know to be true or witnessed himself."

"I believe that," I added for Dylan's assurance. "Jim not only wanted but needed this book to be the truth."

"Exactly," Diana confirmed. "What I did, along with the writer helping me, was to refine Jim's words – edit when necessary. Eliminate any repetition, correct grammar, and make sure that it flowed. These were things Jim and his editor would have eventually done if he had lived to complete it."

"But, when will I be able to see it?" Dylan asked again.

"GG said the press copies had already arrived and they look great," she shared. "I'll check it out as soon as I get back, place an order, and then give you each an advance copy."

"You mean it's there now?" Dylan asked excitedly. "Can I pick up a copy as soon as we get back?"

"No," Diana said sharply. "I need to see it and make sure it's ready before any copies go out."

"When are you coming back?" Trevor asked.

"Wednesday or Thursday?" Diana answered as a question while looking at me.

"Whatever you say," I responded. "As long as Mike is okay."

"Speaking of which," Dylan said as Mike joined us, taking a seat in the arm chair next to the sofa.

"Well?" Diana asked.

"He's going to write a cease-and-desist letter," Mike shared. "He also suggested that I get a restraining order on her."

"It might not do any good, but at least if she breaks it, you can have her arrested," Diana explained. "After all, she did threaten you when she vandalized your car."

"When is all of that going to happen?" Trevor asked.

"GG said he'd get on it right away – before the day is out," Mike replied. Then, turning to Diana, he added: "I don't know what power you have over him but thank you."

"He just knows how I get when things don't happen in a timely manner," Diana joked.

"So, basically, he's afraid of you," said Dylan.

"Something like that," she replied with an evil grin. "Okay, I'm off to check on the camera and RA. She must be bored to tears."

"Actually, she and Karen are out shopping," Dylan shared. "RA sent me a text a little while ago."

"Good. Now you boys stay out of trouble. And Mike, go ahead with that restraining order," Diana instructed. Then, looking at Dylan and Trevor, she added: "I'll see you before you head back."

After Diana left, Mike said that he'd go by the police station once we had lunch. But for now, he wanted to hear Dylan's thoughts about the bar's kitchen. The two of us needed to come up with some sort of concept to appease Peggy.

For the next hour, we discussed Charlie's. Dylan had put a lot of thought into the kitchen expansion, complete with a professional-looking drawing. Trevor also offered good input as we began to lay out the changes. The bar would stay where it was, as well as the jukebox and dance floor.

Expanding the kitchen did affect the booths. Plus, we needed a spot for the piano.

"I'm afraid the number of seats is going to shrink," I began. "Not a problem for the current crowd, but if this takes off, she'll need as many seats as possible."

"The booths aren't anything special," Trevor said. "I know they can be reupholstered, but is it worth it?"

"We have to have some seating with tables," I said. "What's your idea?"

"What about a banquette that runs down that long wall with tables and chairs in front of it?" Trevor suggested. "It would make it easier to see the piano player."

"I like the look, but it doesn't offer privacy for individual groups like a booth would," Mike remarked.

"How much privacy do you have in a booth with another on each side of you?" Dylan asked. "This way, it would bring everyone together and not divided by sections."

"I think there should also be a few two-top or four-top tables with chairs in front of the piano," Trevor added.

"And the piano in the corner against the new kitchen wall?" Mike asked.

"Yes," I agreed. "Then, one-third of the room is open for standing."

"From the front door to where the bar begins will be left open for standing and mingling. The booths or banquette would then start along the wall ending at the new bumped-out kitchen wall. Dining tables with chairs would be placed between the booths and the bar," Mike explained.

"You could also add a few bistro cocktail tables to set drink glasses on," Trevor suggested.

"What about a mirrored wall behind the piano?" Dylan asked.

"With sconces," Trevor added. "On a dimmer, of course."

"I think there should be tablecloths on the nights the piano player is there," I remarked. "With those votives that are the LED flameless kind. Not real ones, or some queen would catch her boa on fire and burn the place down."

While we were talking, Mike had been busy sketching the room to scale, putting tables and chairs as we had talked about.

"I'm coming up with seating for forty," he said. "That's not a lot, especially if you're serving dinner."

"Actually, for the size of the kitchen, that's not bad,"

Dylan said.

"Okay, back up," I interrupted as an idea popped into my head. "Could the booths be pulled apart and placed end to end to create the banquette? That would save a lot of money."

"And is the upholstery in bad condition or just bland?" Mike asked. "We need to look at it closely because it might work."

"It doesn't give us more seating, though," I remarked.

"You could do two seatings a night. Maybe an early show around seven, and another at nine," Trevor suggested.

"And small plates – appetizers for the late show," Dylan commented.

"I'm not sure if their plan is for scheduled shows or just have someone playing, taking a break, the jukebox takes over, and then back at it," Mike said. "I guess a lot will depend on the chef and the entertainment."

"You do realize that Peggy and Maggie would love for you to consider the position?" I said, breaking the ice. "It would be like your own restaurant."

"We thought that was where this was going," Dylan admitted. "Peggy is not very subtle."

"True," I agreed. "But she has a heart of gold."

"Let's see if she makes a proposal," Trevor said.

"You mean you'd consider it? Both of you?" Mike asked.

"It's either both or nobody," Dylan stated. "Definitely something to think about. I have a good job, but I don't see it advancing. And, as much as I'd love to own a restaurant, the thought of it is scary – the expense and everything that's involved. I remember getting mad at Jim for acting as the voice of reason when I first mentioned the idea. But he was right. It's a huge undertaking."

"I think you're being very wise," I said.

"How about some lunch?" Mike suggested. "We've got a great Thai place close by."

"That sounds perfect," Dylan replied. "What about the others?"

"I can shoot them a group text," Trevor offered as Mike and I groaned.

"What?" he asked.

"Nothing. See who's up for it?" I said, hiding my disdain for group texts.

We got a good response from the others. Karen brought Roberta Ann with her, and Bobby and Gayle came separately.

Peggy said Thai food didn't always agree with her, but she didn't want to be left out. She would pick up Maggie along the way. Val was helping a friend with car troubles, so Char came alone.

Basil was a neighborhood restaurant located in a renovated former fast-food burger joint space. The decor was clean, uncluttered and stylish. The hostess had combined two tables to accommodate our group.

"Where's Diana?" RA asked.

"She's checking on the exterior camera, hoping it caught Ming in action," I began. "And she wanted to stop by the local Bureau office to see if she could find out anything."

"I'm going to get a restraining order against Ming this afternoon," Mike announced. "And Mr. Glitter-Gate himself is writing a cease-and-desist letter. We'll see if that works."

Karen wanted to know about the newspaper article since she had not been there when the call came through. Mike explained what had happened and said he hoped that he put an end to it.

"You threatened to sue the paper and the journalist," Trevor reminded him. "I doubt that they thought you were kidding."

"It just caught me off guard," Mike admitted. "Maybe I overreacted a bit."

"Not at all," Peggy assured him. "You have to stand your ground."

"I'm dying to ask if you guys had a chance to talk this morning about the bar?" Maggie asked. "It's okay if you didn't, with everything going on."

"We did," Mike assured her. "Dylan and Trevor had some great ideas. Ricky and I will work on it tonight.

"Thank you," Peggy added.

"Did you save me anything?" Diana yelled from the front door of the restaurant. "I'm famished."

"I didn't expect you to be done this early," I replied. "What did you find out?"

"Hold your horses, and let me order some lunch. Jeez," she groaned.

Once she placed her order, she told us that the camera did not catch Ming in action, only her walking to and from. However, the timestamp put her there at the right time wearing her stupid animal print coat that the guys had described.

"Does that give them enough to at least question her?" Mike asked.

"It should, although it's not considered a serious crime. Or basically, not worth their time," Diana explained. "No one was hurt. Your insurance will take care of it. Yada, yada, yada."

"What about the Bureau?" RA asked.

"They checked with the local cops to see if they had anything on her and if her name was familiar to them. There had been three complaints over the years accusing her of theft. But nothing amounted to an arrest."

"Then stealing from my mother-in-law wasn't the only time?" Char asked. "I can't wait to tell Val."

"Anything on Gator?" Bobby asked.

"First of all, his real name is Luther. Luther Oman Leatherwood," Diana revealed. "And yes, there was one charge for sexual assault."

"Tell me that wasn't the thing with his son's girlfriend," Mike said.

"No, this was way back before he was married. Fifty-two years ago," Diana explained. "He was twenty-two, but the girl was seventeen."

"Underage," Dylan remarked. "Like me when Matt entered my life."

"Yes," Diana acknowledged. "And, the case had been sealed at one time."

"We graduated high school fifty-two years ago next spring," said Karen. "1970."

"That means Gator was four years older than us?" I commented. "Or five years depending on when his birthday was."

"I wonder if Ming knew about his past," Karen asked. "Maybe not since he had a wife between the assault charge and Ming."

"It makes me curious if maybe there were others who didn't press charges," Dylan added. "Sorry, this is a little too close to home."

Trevor placed his hand on Dylan's, and Peggy gave him a motherly look of concern.

"Now what?" Char asked, breaking the awkward moment.

"I don't know that there is a now what?" Diana said truthfully. "Until Ming commits an actual crime or threat, we're pretty much at a standstill."

"How long had Ming and Gator been married?" asked Karen.

"I think just a little over twenty years," Mike answered. "And, I believe the first marriage lasted about the same. Ming said when she met Gator, his son was eight or nine."

"So, he didn't marry until he was around thirty?" I asked.

"I'm pretty sure he got drafted and served for a few years when he was in his twenties," Mike explained. "The draft was still in effect until 1973. My college sent confirmation that I was a student to keep me from going."

"Same here," I added.

"And Connie?" Gayle asked. "Do we just forget about her?"

"What do you propose, Gayle?" Mike asked a little too sharply. "She doesn't want anything to do with us. Even if Ming did have a gun to her head, she hasn't given us a glimmer of hope that she wants or needs our help. By the way, she's my friend, too."

Seeing Gayle begin to tear up, I realized that we needed a quick change in the conversation.

"Maggie," I began. "Do you live with Peggy, or do you have your own place?"

"I'm renting a little bungalow in the Highlands area near Fourteenth Street. Why?" she replied.

"What if Mike contacted Danny and said he had one more job if Danny was interested. But that he needs to know he can trust him because he doesn't want Ming to interfere."

"And?" Mike asked.

"You give him Maggie's name, phone number, and general area of town. Then we wait and see how long before Ming contacts her," I explained.

"Setting a trap for Danny that you can use to make him tell you what Ming's up to," Diana summarized. "I like it."

"Maggie won't be in any danger, right?" Peggy asked.

"No, he'll only have her phone number," I replied.

"And even that could be a burner phone," Diana added. "And a fake last name."

"I'm game," Maggie said. "If Ming does call, what do I tell her?"

"That Mike said he'd call, or a guy named Danny who he recommended. Then, you ask why she's calling and what her connection to Mike is," RA suggested.

"And, record it!" Dylan added, getting excited.

"Let's say it all happens as planned," Karen began. "Then what do you have?"

"Leverage," Diana answered. "I'd like to talk with Danny at that point about Connie and Ming."

"You want me to play good cop to your bad-ass cop?" Char asked.

"Tempting," Diana replied, smiling. "But I think I might need to do this one alone."

"But Char, you could go ahead and tell Val that you're helping Diana and watch her freak out," Bobby suggested.

"Freak out because she'd be worried?" Trevor asked.

"No, freak out being jealous that Char gets to role-play a cop and not her," Peggy said laughing.

CHAPTER
Twelve

Once lunch was over, I drove Mike and the boys back home. Diana followed, as did Karen with Roberta Ann and her overnight bag. When I turned into Mike's driveway, I came to a sudden stop.

"What the hell?" Trevor exclaimed.

Sitting on the front porch was the floral arrangement that he had delivered to Connie earlier in the day. Trevor jumped out to retrieve it, but Diana, who had pulled in behind us, yelled for him to stop. She motioned for us to pull around to the back as we would normally do. When everyone had parked and gotten out of their cars, she explained why she had stopped Trevor.

"It looks like the same arrangement and probably is harmless," she began. "But we need to be cautious."

"You think Ming put a bomb in it?" Dylan joked.

"I don't know what she did," Diana snapped. "And that's the point. What if there was some kind of acid or accelerant in the vase?"

"Then the flowers would be dead," I remarked.

"Unless there is a vase within a vase," Karen added, catching on.

"I'm going to check," Diana announced. "Go inside and wait."

Diana walked around the house toward the porch as we gathered and watched through the front window. She studied it carefully, pulled out a pen and gently separated the flowers. When she decided it was harmless, she picked up the vase and rang the doorbell to be let in.

"It's fine," she proclaimed. "But wait until you read the note."

Attached was the same card Trevor had tried earlier to get Connie to return with a message. Ming, we assumed, had written a response. "Nice try, Mike. But you might want to save these for your going away party."

"That cow!" Mike yelled.

"That means Connie told her, or Ming was watching from afar," RA said. "You guys have got your hands full. I wish there were something that I could do."

"It means so much that you came to visit this weekend," I said. "All of you."

"Yes, thank you," Mike added. "We'll get this thing sorted out, and maybe your next visit will be drama-free."

"Is there ever such a thing?" Diana joked. "Now, you guys get on the road and don't mess up my car."

We watched as the three of them put their things in the back of Diana's car and with Dylan at the wheel, drove away.

"I guess I should get going, too," Karen said. "Unless there is something that you think I can do to help."

"Not at the moment," Mike replied. "Ricky and I are going to put together a proposal for Peggy. After all, the show must go on!"

"I'll follow you and pick up my stuff," Diana said to Karen. "You have been so gracious in letting us stay with you."

Once again, Diana surprised me with her appreciative comment. I was beginning to think Bellwood might be good for her.

Mike, clearly upset and rightfully so, managed to focus on the task at hand. But, we were still concerned that Ming had been so brazen. Not only to return the arrangement but to bring it to his front door. Did she know that we weren't home? Did she even care? Diana had said earlier that it didn't feel as if Ming wanted a confrontation. But stepping onto Mike's property was not the way to avoid it.

As we discussed the project, we found ourselves excited at the prospect of creating a new Charlie's – fresh yet timeless. We were only able to come up with rough estimates to start. Paint and new lighting was easy. But we had to guess the expense for the commercial appliances and what it might cost to bring everything up to codes.

"If the booths *will* actually turn, line up down the wall, and not need to be reupholstered," I commented, "then, we'll save a bundle."

"Still, we'll need additional tables and definitely new chairs," Mike reminded me.

"Did you like the idea of a mirrored wall and sconces behind the piano?" I asked.

"Yes, but above a chair rail. If it went to the floor, it could be easily broken," Mike explained. "What about an acid wash or foxing on the mirror? It would give an old-world look, reflect light, but not show fingerprints as much."

"And being distorted, queens won't be tempted to check their hair and makeup," I added jokingly.

"I used some recently in an entrance hall," Mike shared. "I think I can estimate based on that job."

"Do you know the width?" I asked. "I didn't think to get measurements."

"After Peggy requested our help, I counted the two-foot by four-foot ceiling tiles one night out of curiosity," Mike admitted. "I think I have a pretty good idea."

"Look at you," I said proudly. "I'm impressed. Even if I had thought to count them, I would have forgotten the number by now."

"Well, you're retired – out of practice," Mike explained, smiling. "I, on the other hand – regardless of what Ming Leatherwood thinks – am still gainfully employed."

Just then, we heard something hit one of the front windows – and then another.

"What the hell was that?" Mike yelled as we rushed toward the front door.

"Don't open it," I barked, motioning for him to join me at one of the living room windows. We watched as two guys jumped into a blue sedan parked on the street. We were too far away to get a description of them or know for sure the make of their nondescript vehicle as it sped away.

"Let's go out the back and walk around to make sure no one was left behind," Mike suggested.

Nothing appeared to be amiss until we saw what had been thrown at the front of Mike's home – two pink plastic water bottles in the shape of penises filled with liquid. I mentioned the added weight would make them easier to throw.

"Don't touch it," I said. "We don't know what's in them, and there might be fingerprints. I'm calling Diana."

Mike sat down on the front steps. The adrenaline rush had faded, and he slumped over as if the weight of the world was on his shoulders.

"Diana called one of her cop buddies who said he'd come by and make a report," I explained.

"Ming?" Mike asked. "I know it wasn't her, but don't you think it was a result of her?"

"How could it not be?" I asked while pulling up Ming's social media page. "Surely, she would not have put your address out there for all to see."

"It wouldn't surprise me," Mike said.

"Not your address, but your business name," I confirmed. "There's a post saying she is taking over your business because homosexuals need to understand they have no place in our world."

"No place in whose world?" Mike asked. "With the name of my business, any moron following her page could look up the address."

"She might not have instructed someone to harass us. And, she might not be aware of what just happened," I said. "But she planted the seed. I wonder how many more of her followers will come after you. The number has grown to over eight hundred."

"I don't want to say anything to the others," Mike announced. "Diana knows, but I don't want to alarm anyone else."

"I'll agree if Diana agrees," I said with reservation.

The officer arrived, took our statements, and removed the bottles. He said he'd check for fingerprints, but like the previous incident, didn't give us much hope. However, he did open one of the bottles and said it appeared to be urine. I asked about DNA, and he smiled before admitting there was a backlog.

Mike was upset but put on a brave front and insisted we get back to work.

We discussed wall and ceiling colors and decided on a deep taupe shade. The bar had gone through several color combinations over the years, but the ceiling tiles had been painted black for as long as Mike could remember. The walls had been tan, navy, deep red, and now a drab shade of gray.

"Weren't the booths originally a tobacco color?" I asked. "1970s Naugahyde®?"

"Good memory," Mike acknowledged. "They had gotten in bad shape, so Peggy had them redone when she inherited the bar. And black is easier to work with."

"Let's see if we can meet up with her and Maggie, take

another look at the place with our design ideas in mind, then present our proposal."

"I'll give Peggy a call right now," Mike offered. "And, then I'll shoot Danny an email about Maggie. I hope that I'm wrong about him helping Ming. He's been a friend and business associate for years."

"The same can be said about Ming," I reminded him. "For whatever reason, people change."

Peggy suggested we meet at seven-thirty allowing us to eat dinner before going. I texted Diana to see if she'd be home to join us. It was already five-thirty, and I was curious if she was on her way. She replied that she had picked up her things from Karen and would be there shortly. We cleaned the bathroom and made ready the guest room that the boys did not use.

Mike emailed Danny and told him that he knew he'd supplied Ming with client information and that he was disappointed with the betrayal. Danny immediately replied on the defensive. He said he couldn't believe he was being accused of such a thing. He said he had no idea that Connie and Jackie would be coming to pick up Ming's things at that time.

We felt Danny could be manipulated easily and was no match for Ming's tactics.

Therefore Mike chose to give him the benefit of the doubt. Ming was aware of Danny's visit and met him at the other designer's studio after he left Mike's. Therefore, she could have easily planned the ambush at Mike's for when Danny would be there without ever telling him.

Mike emailed Danny back to say he had a new job that could turn into something big. One, the client needed draperies, bedspreads, shower curtains, pillows – the works. And, that he had suggested custom mirrors for the baths as well as a large one on the dining room wall. Mike shared that he had found someone to replace Ming but wondered if Danny would be interested in the mirror work. He added that he needed to feel he could trust Danny and didn't want it to get back to Ming. He ended the email with a question. "Can I count on you to keep this to yourself?"

Danny replied wholeheartedly, yes. Mike gave him Maggie's name and phone number to call.

"Want to place a bet on how long it will take before Ming knows?" I asked.

"I hope that you're wrong."

Diana came charging through the back door at six-thirty, yelling at us for not having it locked.

"Are you finished?" Mike asked calmly. "Or, do you need to yell some more?"

Diana looked startled and began to open her mouth.

"Sweetie, it was locked," I began. "We saw your car turn into the drive, and I got up and unlocked it for you."

"If you say so," she replied. "Okay, fill me in."

Mike told her we had the proposal for Charlie's, and she asked about the estimate. He gave her a range since we did not have concrete figures.

"That's not so bad," she said. "I was thinking it might be higher."

"Mike emailed Danny," I continued. "Of course, he denied it, but he took the bait. We're just waiting for Ming to call Maggie."

"What if she says something to Connie?" Diana asked. "Would Connie recognize the name?"

"No way," Mike explained. "I used Margaret instead of Maggie and a different last name."

"You think Connie and Ming are so tight that neither would make a move without the other knowing?" I asked.

"I don't know," Diana began, "but, so far they appear to be connected at the hip."

"It shocks and disappoints me," Mike said with sadness. "I remember when she and Jackie picked up Ming's things. Connie kept saying that she didn't want to be in the middle. And yet she put herself in the middle, didn't she? She could have said no. She could have given me a heads-up they were coming if she felt she had to help Ming. Once you see that side of a person, it's hard to un-see it. I'll never trust her again. I don't even know that I'll be comfortable talking about anything in front of her. And I have no idea what that will do with my relationship with Gayle. All because Ming has poisoned them with her lies."

"Not that it's the same thing, but after seeing the political comments from a few friends on social media, I felt the same. Like I couldn't *not* see it. They had shown me who they were – what they thought – and their stance against our freedoms. I saw what was in their hearts," I added.

"Do you want to talk about the pink penis bottle incident?" Diana said to Mike. "I'll admit that was a first for me."

"You think it's the sort of thing that happens to us often?" Mike responded tersely.

"No, of course not," Diana replied. "I didn't mean to sound like I take it lightly. It was an aggressive move that was either instigated or ignited by Ming's post."

"I told Ricky that I don't want to say anything to the others," Mike stated. "At least for now. Okay?"

"Yes, for now. People are shits," Diana declared. "What's for dinner?"

I explained that Mike and I were going to meet with Peggy and Maggie at seven-thirty to discuss our ideas for Charlie's. Diana surprised me by wanting to come along. We decided to eat something on the way since no one was in the mood to cook.

"Do you have a Mother Clucker's here? I could go for some chicken," Diana asked.

"No. What about Red Lobster?" Mike suggested. "I think it's all you can eat shrimp night."

"That works!" Diana decreed.

Over dinner, Mike explained his email to Danny and how he made it sound like it could be a big job – not only for him but for someone with Ming's qualifications. He knew it would be too tempting for Danny to pass. But neither of us was sure if he'd reach out to Ming.

"He might think he'd lose the job if he gave Ming the information," I said. "Unless he thought Ming could take the job away from you, and he'd still get to do his part."

"At this point, he would be a fool to trust her," Diana commented. "By the way, I rode out to Ming's house this afternoon. The van was in the drive, so I didn't linger. It looked like she had a barn out back. Does she have animals?"

"She did at one time, so I assume she still does," Mike explained. "But without Gator, she'd need help taking care of them."

"She needs help physically and mentally, if you ask me," I added.

"And you said her workroom is in the basement?" Diana asked, ignoring me.

"Yes. She had two ladies who worked part-time when she'd get a big job," Mike replied. "One was named Barb or Barbara, and I think the other Caroline or Carol-something. I have no idea if they still work there. Maybe they've seen through her act by now."

"Or, maybe they're just like her," Diana said. "Anti-vaxxer conspiracy theory crackpots with mean streaks."

"I know I keep saying this, but I still don't see what she and Connie have in common," Mike added. "Connie has children and grandchildren. Ming has always despised kids. She'd be the first to beat the crap out of anyone who'd hurt an animal, – but a child, she could not care less."

"What an awful thing," Diana commented. "I don't have kids, but I'd do everything in my power to protect a child as well as an animal, from abuse. She must have zero empathy. Maybe that's why she identifies with the previous President."

"Unless you're planning on another round of shrimp, we should probably go meet up with Peggy and Maggie," I said as Diana grabbed one more cheese biscuit for the road.

CHAPTER
Thirteen

It was a Monday, and the bar wasn't open. Several of the shops in the strip had already closed for the day, except for the Chinese take-out restaurant and a cash checking business on the corner. Peggy had the door locked but opened it as soon as we knocked.

"Were you waiting by the door?" Mike asked.

"Yes, with my heart fluttering in anticipation," Peggy snarked with a laugh.

"Hi Maggie," Mike said, ignoring Peggy. "At least it's good to see you."

"Thank you," she said sweetly. "I didn't expect you, Diana, what a nice surprise. Are there any new developments?"

"Not really," Diana replied. "I suppose you heard about

the flowers being returned."

"That's one brazen heifer," Peggy said.

"On that, we can agree," I added.

"Will you give us a few minutes to look at everything carefully before we start?" Mike asked. "Some of this we were doing from memory. I just need to take a few measurements and look at the booth situation."

"Situation?" Peggy repeated. "We have a situation?"

"Shh! Let them do their thing," Maggie said to her aunt.

"I take it you haven't gotten a call about design work, have you?" Diana asked Maggie.

"Not yet," she answered. "I'm kind of nervous and afraid I'll give myself away."

"You'll be fine," Mike said, overhearing their conversation.

We took measurements from where the wall would need to be moved out for the kitchen expansion. Mike was spot on with his counting – ceiling – tiles measuring. All of the booths looked in good condition – no tears or worn areas. They separated easily, which meant our idea of lining up the booths could work and be very economical.

"Are you ready?" Mike asked.

Peggy responded with: "Yes, but please be gentle."

"When was the last time you said that?" I asked Diana.

"That would be never," she answered, laughing.

"Behave!" Mike scolded us.

Maggie had pulled a table out of a booth and put four chairs from the back hall around it. She retrieved one more chair for Diana and added it to the table. We began talking about our ideas and even got up to point and demonstrate our thoughts. Then Mike rolled out the rough to-scale drawing to show them.

"I like the idea of the banquette," Maggie said. "Even though it won't take up less room when you put a table and chairs opposite it. I think the room will appear more open."

"And make it easier for everyone to see the piano player," Mike added.

"Will that be enough seating as well as enough overflow standing room?" Peggy asked.

"It's about the same either way," I replied."Booths or banquette. Of course, we want a few free-standing tables and chairs."

"Won't they be in the way?" Maggie asked.

"We'll position them closer to the banquette than the bar,"

Mike explained. "That way, someone could be seated at the bar with a couple of friends standing behind them and people will still be able to pass by for the restrooms, and the servers going to the kitchen."

"And the people standing in the back should be far enough away from the piano so as not to be a distraction," I added.

"One thing the boys brought up: whether you'd have a pianist play, take a break, then play some more, with customers gathering around the piano to sing along," Mike began.

"Or," I continued, "have a set time for a show. You know, like a seven o'clock show and then maybe a nine or nine-thirty one."

"Would that make a difference?" Peggy asked.

"Dylan was thinking about food service," I explained. "Maybe a dinner menu at seven and then small plates and appetizers later on."

"Why?" Maggie asked.

"Limited kitchen space, I think," Mike said. "Limited number of meals that can be served. You know, food on hand."

"I see," Peggy said. "Lots to think about. We definitely may need to start small and go from there. The dinner menu could be limited. Maybe three options nightly, and those could change seasonally. I guess it would be a decision for whoever we hire as chef."

"But you want Dylan, don't you?" I asked. "You'd like him to move here and work for you?"

"Were we that obvious?" Maggie asked.

"How can I put this delicately? Duh!" I said. "But they might be open to it, depending on your proposal."

"They?" Peggy asked. "You mean Trevor is willing to come, too?"

"You're the one who pulled them aside and said not to let anything or anyone come between them," I reminded her. "Of course, they're a package deal."

"That's so exciting," Peggy said, smiling. "Talk to me about money. How much is this redo going to cost me? That will determine what I can offer them to start. I know that once it takes off, money shouldn't be an issue. But, at the start, it's my bank account that's going to pay for the remodeling and his salary – along with bartenders and servers."

Mike explained where we saved her money first. Then the paint, lighting, tables, chairs, and construction of the wall.

The unknown was the kitchen equipment, although we had a rough estimate.

"Jesus," Peggy sighed. "I know you've done it as economically as you could, but that is pretty much what I thought I could spend for everything. The piano would then be on top of that. There's no way that I could make Dylan an offer tempting enough to leave Hillmont. There would be nothing left. Where can we cut?"

"We don't have to paint or change out lighting, I guess. And we can leave the booths as they are and see if we can find some used restaurant equipment," Mike suggested.

"You've got to have the piano, and if you're going to do food and hire Dylan, then you need to give him a functional kitchen," I added.

"That sucks," Maggie said with frustration. She then turned to Peggy and added: "I'm not saying that to make you feel bad. You're willing to sink your own money into making this happen. I had just hoped that when we reopened that it would be with a new look. Something for the old-timers to enjoy and the new kids to think is fresh and happening."

"We talked about a possible online fundraising campaign," I reminded them.

"Do you seriously think that many people would contribute?" Peggy asked. "There are two other bars in town that are already fresh and happening, as Maggie said."

"I know you're disappointed," Mike said sincerely. "Let us work on it again. Get actual quotes, and..."

Maggie's phone rang, and a look of panic appeared on her face.

"It's her," she said. "This is the burner, so it has to be her. What do I do?"

"Give it to me," Diana ordered.

Maggie passed the phone to Diana as if it were a hot potato. Diana clicked and calmly said, "Hello."

"Yes, this is she," she continued. "I'm sorry. Who did you say you were?"

I don't think any of us had taken a breath.

"I'm not sure I understand," Diana said. "I was expecting Mike to call me. Or, wait a sec, yes, here it is – some guy named Danny."

"Uh-huh. I see." She continued playing along. "So you

work for Mike? No? You're taking over his design business? I'm confused. I just hired him, and he didn't mention that he was retiring."

Maggie and Peggy looked at us, and we all turned back to watch Diana in action.

"I think I need to speak with Mike. After all, you don't know what we've discussed. Oh, you do?"

This was getting good now.

"Yes, that's right. Uh-huh. Yes. Well, I guess he has discussed it with you. I'm just surprised that he didn't tell me. That's a poor way to handle his business. Oh, you're right. It's now your business. I certainly hope you do better to than him."

I could see Mike getting touchy, even though it was all make-believe.

"My address?" Diana asked. "He didn't even tell you where I live?"

Diana began flailing her arms, motioning to give her an address. Peggy grabbed my pen and wrote down hers, which Diana read off to Ming.

"Tomorrow? Sure, that will work. Ten o'clock?"

Diana looked at Peggy, and she nodded yes.

"Fine, I'll see you then."

"Are you sure, Peggy?" Diana asked when she disconnected the call.

"Better have the psycho come to me than to Maggie," Peggy replied.

"For God's sake, what did she say?" Mike yelled.

"Dial it back a notch, will ya?" Diana joked.

Diana explained that Ming was very business-like but slightly pushy. Trashed Mike for being no longer interested or up on design trends. Said she had worked with him briefly to get the lay of the land before buying his business. She was shocked that he had even met with a client when he knew he wasn't going to actually do the job. But that he had done that a couple of times before.

"That skanky pile of..." Mike began as his face turned red.

"Settle down," Peggy said calmly. "That's not going to do anyone any good."

"Thank you," Diana said sincerely. "I'm going to meet her in the morning. I don't have any jurisdiction here and can't hold her or arrest her. She might walk out, or she might decide she's up for the challenge. But, I can explain what will happen if she continues down this road."

"I want to be there," Mike said.

"I don't think that you could remain calm. And if you got out of line, she could use it against you," Diana warned.

"I can stay calm," Mike pleaded, with no encouragement from the rest of us.

"What if we were in another room listening and promised not to make a sound?" I asked.

"I don't think that's possible," Diana replied. "But I also don't think she'll be there long. My main purpose is to let her know that an agent with the Bureau is onto her."

"That would scare most people," I admitted. "I'm not sure it will even faze her."

"It's funny that, when you step away from a relationship, you actually see it clearer," Mike began. "I think back on some of Ming's hostile actions towards others. How she could be dismissive and condescending, especially to women. At the trade shows, I'd have someone pull me aside and ask why she was rude to them. Some would jokingly say she scared them, but I think there was some truth to that. Since it wasn't directed at me, I didn't take it seriously. I now know that I should have – I should have called her out on it."

"Do you think it would have made a difference?" Maggie asked.

"Probably not," Mike admitted. "She's a bully, always has been, and now her wrath is aimed at me."

"While we've got Maggie and Peggy here," I began, "let's talk about what to do next with Charlie's."

"One more thing, if I may," Diana said as we all turned toward her. "How much more do you think you'll go over your estimate? I know you have a rough idea of the kitchen expense, but do you think it could be $10,000 more? $20,000 more?"

"I don't know for sure and would hate to guess wrong. But, if I had to answer right this very minute, I'd say $20,000 should be enough and hopefully provide a little cushion in case we're off on anything else," I said, as Mike nodded in agreement.

"So, you're comfortable with your original estimate plus $20,000?" she asked.

"I'm not," Peggy jumped in before we could answer. "That would be practically everything I could come up with. No cushion for me. No chef's salary. No piano. No money to pay a piano player."

"That's the dream figure, Peggy," Mike said, trying to calm her. "We'll trim it down as much as possible."

I could see Maggie struggling not to look disappointed. She was torn between wanting to do it right but not bankrupting her aunt.

"Maybe this was just a dream," Peggy said with resolve. "We tried, and it's a great idea, but I don't think I can pull it off. I'll keep Charlie's going for as long as I can."

"How much is the piano?" Diana asked.

"They said we could have it for $5,000," Peggy answered. "I don't even know what a pianist would expect to make. Or, for that matter, a chef."

"I know what Dylan brings home now," Diana said, surprising us. "He told Jim, and Jim told me."

Diana gave Peggy the figure, and Peggy thought she could match that and then some. But, if Trevor were a waiter, his pay would need to be the same as everyone else.

Although, she did say he should be able to do well with tips. Maggie offered to ask Victor at the piano store what he thought would be a fair wage – either an hourly rate or nightly rate.

Dollar amounts were coming and going, and I could see Peggy getting more and more alarmed at the proposed overhead. If she had thought it through from the start, she must have underestimated everything. Or never totaled it all together.

"So now we have the original amount, plus $20,000, plus $5,000 for the piano. Then, we have Dylan's salary and a piano player's fee. As far as bartenders, servers and such, you're already handling that, so that's not a new expense," Diana summarized.

Peggy looked like she had been beaten down, reminding me of how her life had been before Charlie's. It broke my heart. I wanted so badly to help.

"I'm sorry I've wasted everyone's time," she said softly.

"Is that any way for the Alpha of the Bellwood family to act?" Diana asked. "Never let them see you look down and defeated. Do you hear me?"

"Yes," Peggy answered. "You're right. It will be okay. We'll figure something out."

"What you need to figure out is how soon you can get started," Diana said, as we all thought we had heard her wrong.

"Get started?" Maggie asked.

"My best friend Jim left me in charge of his estate with firm directions that the money had to be used to help someone in need. It had to make a difference in someone's life. And to let it do good," Diana announced. "I'm writing you a check for everything but payroll. That's on you. So you better get this thing off the ground and invite me for the grand reopening."

Peggy and Maggie were in tears and excitedly hugged each other. Then they went in for the kill, hugging Diana.

"Okay, settle down. Let's not get crazy," Diana said.

"Shut up!" Peggy snapped. "This is what happens when good happens."

Mike and I were tearing up. "Are you sure?" I foolishly asked.

"Seriously, you're not questioning me, are you?" Diana replied sharply.

"No, ma'am," I said apologetically. "You really are something, you know. I see why Jim loved you so."

With tears beginning to flow, Diana got up from the table

and turned her back to wipe her eyes. When she turned around, she said: "It's time to go. We've got a busy morning taking down the fake-name-floozie. I want to be there by nine so she doesn't see me arriving and get spooked."

"I can't believe you would do this for us," Maggie said.

"I'm not doing anything," Diana corrected her. "This is a gift from the James Norris Foundation. I'd prefer that you go along with your original plan. Let everyone assume it's all your investment. I, along with the foundation, prefer to remain anonymous."

Peggy gave her one more hug, and Diana gave into it this time.

"Thank you, and get some rest," Maggie said as we walked to our car.

When Maggie closed the bar door, we could hear the two of them scream with excitement. I looked at Diana and started to say something, but she put up her hand to stop me.

"Don't," Diana said, in a tone that let me know this conversation was over.

CHAPTER

Fourteen

The next morning the three of us drove over to Peggy's in Diana's rental car. Peggy lived in a modest home on a quiet street in an average neighborhood. The exterior was well-kept, and the yard was nicely landscaped. However, it was not the size home that would need the amount of work Ming would be expecting. I mentioned that as a concern, but Diana shrugged it off and said it wouldn't matter.

We circled the area before parking to make sure we didn't see Ming's van. Peggy ushered us inside and seemed surprised that Diana had let Mike and me come. And we were surprised to see Maggie there as well. But, as it turned out, there was another surprise that we had not counted on.

"I am dead serious that you guys can't make a sound," Diana instructed. "She is probably going to be hypersensitive to everything around her. And, as lovely as your home is, I'm sure she will be curious after I made it sound like a much larger undertaking."

"We can wait in the kitchen and still be able to hear your conversation," Peggy suggested. "I'm assuming you won't be giving her a tour."

"I plan to make my point first thing, catching her off guard," Diana explained. "She'll either rise to the occasion or hightail it out of here. I can't legally make her stay and listen, so I'll be moving fast and hard from the start."

"Will you eventually let her know that we're here?" Mike asked.

"I'll just have to play it by ear," she replied. "If I do, I'd rather she didn't know that Peggy and Maggie are here. I'm assuming she doesn't know you, and it should stay that way."

"I may have mentioned Peggy at some point," Mike explained. "But, as far as I know, she has never been in Charlie's to be able to recognize them."

"She can find out whose house this is from the property tax records," I pointed out. "That is if she hasn't already done so."

"If she has and thinks it's a trap," Diana added, "then she probably won't show at all."

"It's a quarter til," Maggie announced. "We ought to take our places in case she's early. We wouldn't want her to hear us scrambling to hide."

The four of us went into Peggy's neat-as-a-pin kitchen. She had a table with four chairs in front of a window overlooking her backyard. But Mike and I stood near the bi-fold door so as not to miss a thing.

"You're going to have to back up, guys," Diana said once we shut the door. "There's light coming through the crack, and it's flickering with your movement."

"Is that better?" Mike asked as we joined Maggie and Peggy at the table.

"Yes," Diana said. "I'm recording this in case you miss anything."

Just then, the doorbell rang, and those of us in the kitchen froze in place. I heard Diana open the door and invite Ming in.

"Hi, I'm Ming Leatherwood, and this is my associate, Connie," Ming said loud and clear.

"Connie?" Mike silently mouthed with eyes opened wide.

"Please come in and have a seat," Diana offered.

"Thank you," Ming replied. "You have a lovely home. I have to ask if this is the home you were referring to for design work?"

"Before I answer," Diana began, "may I ask you a question?"

"Of course," Ming replied politely.

"Are you familiar with *Peeper*, the novel that came out last year?" she asked.

"I wasn't expecting that," Ming answered. "What an unusual question. But to answer you, I'm aware of it and all the scandal that came out, but I haven't read it."

"That's disappointing," Diana said.

"Is this a test?" Ming asked. "I *am* familiar with the story, though. A peeping pervert wrote about his sick gay fantasies and pretended it was fiction. He was trying to get away with being something he wasn't."

"Which was?" Diana replied.

"Normal, I guess," Ming answered. "But his lies caught

up with him, didn't they? Someone murdered him. It's surprising that it didn't happen sooner."

Mike and Peggy put their hands on mine to keep me from charging in there and kicking Ming to the curb.

"Did I pass your test?" Ming inquired with a bit of attitude.

"What about you, Connie?" Diana asked, ignoring Ming.

"Yes, I've read it," she replied. "A friend of a friend knew the gentleman who wrote it."

"Gentleman?" Ming repeated with a laugh.

Ignoring her, Diana asked Connie if she remembered the character in the book named Donna.

"Oh yes, the one who turned out to be an agent for the State Bureau of Investigations," Connie answered excitedly.

"Good," Diana remarked. "Her character was based on me."

The room got very quiet. The four of us in the kitchen held our breath waiting to find out what was happening.

"So, Margaret, is it?" Ming began. "You're in law enforcement?"

"Correct," Diana replied. "Is that a problem?"

"No, not at all," Ming answered unconvincingly. "But,

maybe we should talk about what your design needs are, as Connie and I are limited on time."

"I spoke with Mike, and he said he did not sell his business to you. Or, for that matter, give it to you. In fact, he said he no longer works with you," Diana began. "Plus, he was baffled why you'd email his clients and say differently. He even said the newspaper contacted him to verify a story they were doing on you. But, he was able to set them straight."

"He's confused," Ming said nervously.

"I think I should go," Connie added.

"Not just yet," Diana said sharply. "Because my understanding is that you're Ms. Leatherwood's accomplice. Did you know that she vandalized Mike's car the other night? A security camera was able to catch her in the act."

"That's a lie," Ming snapped back. "There is no way that camera saw me."

"Thank you for your confession," Diana said smugly. "I now have it recorded."

"What?" Ming asked defiantly.

"And didn't you just receive a letter to cease-and-desist from Mike's attorney, George Grant?" Diana asked. "But here you are committing fraud – pretending to be something you're not. You do remember what happened to the author of *Peeper*? As you said, 'trying to get away with something that he wasn't.' Didn't you just comment about his murder that you were surprised it didn't happen sooner?"

"Come on, Connie, we're going," Ming said, and we could hear movement.

"I thought you and Mike were friends, Connie," Diana continued. "All the way back to junior high. What could he have possibly done that would cause you to join forces with this whacko?"

"He's an awful man," Connie tried to explain. "He treats his clients terribly. Many of them have complained to Ming about him. They're thrilled she has taken over his business. And for the record, he's the one who's lying. He gave his business to Ming, and now he wants it back. He has taken advantage of her at a time when she's vulnerable. You know her husband just died."

"Funny that you mention 'taken advantage' and 'her husband' together," Diana said. "Did you know that Gator was arrested years ago for taking advantage of an underage girl?"

"That's not true," Ming yelled. "He would never take advantage of anyone. Never force himself on anyone."

"How do you know?" Diana asked. "You weren't married to him at the time. In fact, you're the second wife. The one with whom he had an affair with while he was married with a kid at home."

"You... you don't know what you're talking about," Ming stuttered.

"I know that it was a sad and senseless death. If only he had been vaccinated against COVID," Diana commented.

Ming yelled, "The vaccine is a hoax. They've lied to us."

"And you understand all about lies, don't you?" Diana said.

"May we go?" Connie asked calmly.

"Yes, but just one more question for you," Diana continued. "Did you ask Mike about these accusations? He's been your friend for fifty years. And this woman for what – a couple of years?"

"I know what I know and have no need to talk with him," Connie stated.

"That's a shame," Diana said. "Because he's here. Mike? Will you come in here, please?"

Mike and I stepped out of the kitchen, leaving Maggie and Peggy in place as Diana had suggested. Mike was stunned and hurt. I was so pissed off that I couldn't see straight.

"Why?" was all that Mike had the strength to say.

"Let's go, Connie," Ming said, taking her arm. "He's not worth it."

Connie and Ming left, and then Peggy and Maggie joined us.

"Connie knows the truth but won't let herself accept it," Peggy said, putting her hand on Mike's shoulder. "Just like those cult followers of the last President. They hear with their own ears, see with their own eyes, but refuse to believe it."

"What can you do now?" Maggie asked Diana.

"Not much," she replied. "We don't have video of her actually committing the vandalism, but we do have her admitting to it. Like I said earlier, it's not that big of a deal for them to pursue it."

"And the letter from the attorney?" Peggy asked. "Can it be enforced?"

"No. It's not a legally binding document," Diana explained. "Mike would have to take her to court, and if his lawsuit is successful, the court might issue a legally binding order."

"So basically, we bluffed, and she has called us on it," Mike said.

"Something like that," Diana replied. "I'm sorry."

"Now that Ming has gotten away with everything, what's to stop her from continuing?" I asked.

"Nothing," Diana admitted. "If she escalates, she might do something arrest-worthy that could put her away."

"But no one wants this to escalate," Maggie said what we were all thinking.

"We need GG to suggest a personal injury lawyer for you," Diana said to Mike.

"So you're thinking this is more of a civil case?" I asked.

"She vandalized your car and is coming after your business – your property in a sense," Diana explained. "The attorney could send a letter demanding payment or some kind of remedy. If Ming didn't respond appropriately, they could file a lawsuit on your behalf."

"A civil suit?" Maggie asked.

"We'll need to talk with GG first. But yes, I think that would be the next move," Diana stated.

"I'm so sorry about Connie," I said, changing the subject. "She's gone to the dark side for now. Maybe she'll come to her senses and make things right."

"I'm not sure I even care," Mike said. "She can apologize, and I can say I forgive her, but it's not the same. I don't see her as my friend anymore."

"Why on earth would Connie believe anything coming out of that woman's mouth?" Maggie asked. "She's evil."

"Speaking of which," I reminded him. "Danny. For whatever reason, he gave you up. You need to ask him to pick up his inventory and then cut him loose."

"Time to clean house," Diana suggested.

"I am so disappointed in Connie," Peggy added. "I wanted to think this would all blow over. But, it's like she is digging in her heels and going all-in on Ming's narrative."

"We'll get out of your hair," Mike said to Peggy. "Thank you for letting us use your home today. That means so much."

"I'm glad I could help," Peggy replied. "And I'm glad that I could witness it firsthand. It's still sad, but it makes it easier to let Connie go."

Once we were in the car, I asked if we should get lunch while we were out. I didn't think any of us were hungry, but we needed a diversion. Mike suggested a meat and three spot similar to where we'd go with Jeff in Hillmont.

"Good choice," Diana said. "I could use something healthy in my body."

"May I ask you about Jim's foundation?" I gently inquired.

"I've been waiting for this," Diana acknowledged.

"What exactly is it, and what were Jim's instructions?" I bravely asked.

"At the time of his death, Jim didn't know if the book would be successful or what kind of money it could generate. He did know that his biggest assets were his condo and his car, both of which were paid in full. And there were a few investments as well," Diana explained.

"But the book has done well?" Mike asked. "And I imagine the next one will be a hit, too."

"I can only hope," Diana shared. "Jim didn't leave anything to a charity or organization. He asked that a nonprofit foundation be formed to distribute his estate to anyone who I saw struggling and in need of assistance.

The only stipulation was that it be LGBTQ-related, whether an individual or business."

"So, Charlie's met the criteria?" I asked.

"Yes, it's LGBTQ friendly," Diana began. "Although it's not owned by someone who is gay, it still serves the community, including patrons and employees. Plus, if Maggie eventually takes over, then it will have a lesbian owner."

"When did you know that you were going to help them?" Mike asked.

"It doesn't matter," Diana said.

"It does to me," Mike replied. "I'm curious what made you want to help."

"It was on that first day when we had the Q&A session between the Bellwood and the Hillmont families," Diana explained. "The connection that all of you have. The love and respect, as well as concern for each other. It reminded me so much of what we had begun back home. Except you guys go back decades. We only had a couple of years with Jim and Jeff. We'll never have the chance to have what you have. That's when I knew that I wanted to help you."

"We lost a big part of our hearts with Jim and Jeff," I said.

"Now, we need to make sure not to lose each other."

After lunch, Diana dropped us off at the house. She said she wanted to go by the police station to see if she could light a fire under them to bring Ming in for questioning.

Mike emailed Danny to inform him that, since he could no longer trust him, he should pick up his mirrors next time he was in Bellwood. Danny, realizing he bet on the wrong horse, replied that he'd ask a friend to pick them up and store them until he could come to town. Danny handled it well once he knew it was over, which we both appreciated. He sent a follow-up email telling us who and when they would be picking up his inventory. Mike thanked him and wished him the best.

"I don't think Danny has a mean or spiteful bone in him," Mike said to me. "I think Ming manipulated him, and now he's paying the price. Collateral damage."

"Let's go to the store and get groceries," I suggested. "I feel like cooking, and I think we could enjoy an evening at home. Then later, if you want, we could go to Charlie's."

"That sounds good," Mike replied. "I know you and Diana need to go home. And I think we've done all that we can do for now. You don't need to babysit me."

"I'm not. I enjoy being here with you and I worry about you," I admitted. "I'll leave it up to Diana as to when we go back."

Mike and I shopped and brought home way too much from the store. But it felt good doing something normal. I had decided on Chicken Parmesan over spaghetti, a mixture of green vegetables and a Caesar salad. We also bought a fresh baguette from a local bakery and tiramisu for dessert.

"You want to use Bobby's bouquet on the table?" I asked.

"Aren't you hilarious?" Mike replied sarcastically.

When I heard Diana's car pull around to the back, I immediately locked the door. We stood there waiting as she tried the knob and then banged on the door.

"Who's there?" I asked while Mike was trying to suppress laughter.

"Open the G.D. door, Prissy" she yelled.

"Prissy what?" I replied.

"Prissy Pilferer," she snapped and then started laughing.

I opened the door, and Diana charged through, ready for battle. However, she suddenly stopped and asked: "What the hell smells so good? My mouth is already watering."

"Oh, that," Mike said nonchalantly, "dinner."

"What can I do to speed this along?" Diana asked. "Set the table?"

"Done," I replied. "And dinner should be ready in a few minutes. Care for a glass of wine?"

"I could get used to this," she admitted as I handed her a Chardonnay. "I didn't have any luck with the cops, other than I have Ming on their radar in case anything else pops up."

"Mike took care of the Danny situation," I informed her. "He's having a friend pick up his things."

"Good," Diana replied. "You don't need him, especially if you can't trust him."

"We're thinking about going to Charlie's tonight to bring everyone up to speed. Plus, I'm sure Peggy is anxious to share her good news," Mike said.

"Good news that I had nothing to do with, right?" Diana said as a warning.

"Right," I answered.

After dinner, Diana admitted that she didn't know what else she could do for Mike. And that she was anxious to get home and see the proof copies of the new book. Mike agreed and encouraged us to go. He thanked Diana for everything she had done for him, for Charlie's and for his friends. I still felt unsure about leaving him, but like Diana, I was at a loss as to what else could be done.

CHAPTER

Fifteen

Peggy asked us all to stop by Charlie's tonight around eight. She said that she had big news and juicy gossip. We didn't learn until we got there that Gayle wouldn't be joining us. She had not felt good for a couple of days and tested positive for COVID.

Fortunately, she had gotten her shots and booster, but it still had knocked her off her feet, and she was quarantining.

"Should we be concerned?" Val asked. "We've all been around her in the last few days."

"And now we're back together again," Char said.

"Have you seen the news about the new variant?" Karen asked. "It's even more contagious. But if you've had the vaccinations, most likely you won't need to be hospitalized."

"I haven't watched the news in several days," Mike admitted. "I've been too consumed with the whole Ming – Connie – Danny thing."

"Speaking of which," Peggy began, "we had some major drama in my living room this morning."

"Do you think we need to start requiring masks again?" Maggie asked. "At least with the employees?"

"I don't know," Peggy said. "Anyway, Ming showed up, and Connie was with her."

"Connie?" Karen asked. "Gayle never got together with her, did she?"

"No," I answered.

"Good, then Connie didn't catch it," Karen continued.

"Did you hear anything I just said?" Peggy snapped. "Connie was with Ming in my house this morning. She heard Diana lay it all out as to what Ming had been doing, and she didn't care. She wouldn't give Mike a chance to defend himself. We've lost her."

"That can't be true," Val said. "She'll be back."

"No, I don't think she will," Mike said. "And if she is, I will probably have to bow out."

"What are you talking about?" Bobby asked. "She's our friend – your friend for fifty-plus years. You can't turn your back on her."

"Turn my back?" Mike said loudly.

"That's what it sounds like," Karen added.

"You know how Connie reacted after the confrontation this morning? She blocked me from all of her social media pages," Mike said, surprising me. "She's done with me."

"You just need to give her more time to come around," Char suggested.

"No, I don't," Mike stated matter-of-factly.

Val began to say something, but Diana shut her down. Then Karen opened her mouth.

"Shut up," Diana said in a tone that made everyone freeze. "Just shut the fuck up."

I had no idea what was going to happen next, but I was on Team Diana all the way.

"Are you listening to yourselves?" she began. "Peggy and Mike just told you that Connie is so far up Ming's ass that she doesn't know her own name. She has been fed lies and is either foolish enough or just plain stupid enough to believe them without question. I presented proof of Ming's actions to her this morning. She didn't want to hear it. Didn't want to believe it. And more importantly, wouldn't listen to Mike, who was standing right there in front of her."

"Diana, it's okay," Mike said.

"No, it's not," she continued. "You've got something special with your friendships – a bond, as well as history. Maybe Connie will wake up and apologize, or maybe she won't. But right now, you've got this lovely man with a big heart that's breaking right here in front of you. Don't you dare jump on him and act like this is his fault. Do you hear me? Life's too short. You've already lost two friends that you'll never get back. And, you may lose another in Connie. Don't push Mike away. Support each other, dammit."

Everyone in the bar had stopped what they were doing, and you could have heard a pin drop on the carpeted floor. Then, one by one, those who had just witnessed Diana have the perfect Julia Sugarbaker moment began to applaud. Peggy stood up and joined in, followed by Maggie, then Bobby, Val, Char, Karen and myself.

At first, Diana was embarrassed by her outburst, but then smiled and gave her best homecoming queen wave.

Val, who was at least twenty years older than Diana, said: "I want to be like you when I grow up."

"Careful what you wish for," Diana replied. "Now, as you were saying, Peggy."

Peggy finished the story of Ming and Connie from this morning. The disappointment that Ming would get away with her harassment. And the sadness that Connie wouldn't listen to reason. Once she had finished, the others commented, offered suggestions, and ideas – but Diana said none would work and might actually fan the flames.

We talked about Gayle again, wondering if there was something we could do for her. Flowers, food, run errands. Karen said she'd contact her and see if she could find out more. She also said that she'd relay the message about Connie.

"Mike, I think you should share what happened at your house," Diana said. "They need to know."

Mike explained about the urine-filled water-bottle episode. I added that Ming had mentioned Mike's business on her page, and clearly, someone looked up the address and took action.

After Bobby voiced his concern, he shared that Ming's followers had surpassed 1,000 and growing. "She is fueling hate, firing up the masses," Bobby expressed. "Isn't there anything that can be done to stop her?"

"Why would strangers get involved?" Karen asked.

"Like the last President, Ming has given them a reason to let their prejudices and hate shine," Val offered. "To go after a common cause – the Gay Agenda. What's next?"

"You mean, who's next?" Char asked.

"Diana, do you think Mike is in serious danger?" Peggy asked with uneasiness.

"I thought Ming was all bluster," Diana began. "But no one could predict how those paying attention to her rants might act. Or what they could be capable of."

"And somehow Connie is caught up in this," Mike said. "She hasn't given us any indication that she's not or needs our help."

"We need to hear something positive," I said. "Peggy, do you have anything you'd like to tell us?"

"Yes! Maggie and I have good news that we'd like to share

with you," Peggy began. "We have decided to go through with the revamping of Charlie's into a piano bar. I've got the baby grand on hold, and Mike and Ricky have given us a design concept that will refresh the space without losing the charm of our past."

"And we are prepared to make Dylan and Trevor an offer to move to Bellwood and work here," Maggie added. "Dylan would be in charge of the kitchen and menu. We pray that he'll accept."

"That's incredible," Bobby said. "I'm amazed that with everything that's been going on, you've been able to even think about this."

"When will you start?" Val asked. "And how long will you be closed?"

"I'd like to have everything on hand before we start. With the pandemic, it has been difficult to get some things," Mike explained. "Once we have what we need, I think two to three weeks pending inspections."

"Where will we go in the meantime?" Char asked.

"There's always the new leather bar," Bobby joked. "Or the Waffle House out by the interstate."

"It's been a long time since we've done that," Karen said, reminiscing.

"What about the piano player?" Val asked. "Or have you decided on Bobby's twink Victor?"

"He's not a twink, and he's not mine," Bobby quickly corrected her.

"I still think we should place an ad and hold auditions," Maggie said. "We want someone with personality as well as talent. And I agree that we should have a backup plan as well."

"Ricky and I are going back home tomorrow," Diana stated. "I need to see about the book and take care of a few things with Jim's estate."

"And, I need to…" I began.

"Drive me back," Diana finished.

"I'm counting on all of you to take care of Mike," I added. "I doubt that we've heard the last of Ming."

"Don't let down your guard," Diana warned. "Ming may have had a setback today, but that doesn't mean she won't regroup and come after Mike in other ways.

"When will you be back?" Peggy asked. "I kind of like having you around."

"Definitely for the grand reopening of Charlie's, if not before," she answered. "I can't wait to see the changes. When are you going to talk with Dylan?"

"I plan on calling him tomorrow to test the waters," Peggy replied. "I know he'll have to give notice where he works if the answer is yes. And Trevor, too. He may need to sell his house and find something here. It might take longer than we think to pull this off."

"Selling his home will not be a problem in this market," I said. "It might be harder finding something here. He could always rent out his house, but that won't give him a down payment."

"They can stay with me until they find something," Mike offered. "If they say yes, we'll find a way to make it work."

"I wonder if Ming could help them decorate," Val joked as we all groaned. "Too soon?"

"I apologize on behalf of my wife," Char said sincerely.

"In all seriousness, we have a friend who's a realtor that can help," Val added.

"That would be great," said Peggy. "Mike, you better start getting it all together. And Ricky, you're going to help, too?"

"Yes, I'll go home for a few days," I began, "then come back to help Mike since I hear he's retiring."

Mike punched my side and gave me an evil look.

"Too soon?" I asked, then looked at Val and added: "I think it's too soon."

Everyone laughed, and hopefully, it helped Mike to have a little levity. However, I had to admit that if it were happening to me, I doubt I'd handle it as well.

"We have a plan," Peggy said. "Karen is going to check on Gayle and let us know if there is anything that we can do to help. I'm going to call Dylan and pray I can convince him to take a chance with us. Mike is going to start working on the remodel and, then Ricky will be back to help. Diana is going to check on the next book and let us know when it will be ready for us to get our advance copies." Peggy looked at Diana and winked.

"What are we supposed to do?" Val asked.

"Talk to your realtor friend and have them on standby," Peggy said. "If all goes well tomorrow with Dylan, I'll see if I can get an idea of what they might want. A house or condo. And if so, what amenities and price range."

"And I'll figure out how to hold an audition for a pianist," Maggie added.

"But the most important thing is to be careful and avoid Ming," Diana instructed.

"What about me?" Bobby asked.

"You keep tabs on Mike," Peggy instructed. "Stay over if you need to. Don't give Ming another chance to do harm."

We said our goodbyes and I had to admit that I hated to leave. Even though it had been a stressful trip, it felt good being around Mike's friends, who now felt more like my friends – my family as well. My Hillmont family from the Nathaniel days had dwindled to Bill and Greg. I felt grateful to be able to expand my circle of friends. And whether she'd admit it or not, I think Diana felt the same.

Once we were in the car heading home, I shared with Diana that Maggie had pulled me aside to ask just how straight Diana was.

"What did you tell her?" Diana asked out of curiosity.

"As straight as they come," I replied. "That's true, right?"

"Well, there was that one time," she answered with a wicked laugh.

CHAPTER
Sixteen

We got a slow start the next morning, just sitting around drinking coffee and feasting on pancakes and sausage, compliments of Mike.

"I can't remember the last time I had pancakes," Diana said.

"I'm on a sugar high from the syrup and will probably crash within the hour," I added.

"I can see that I'm going to have to drive us home," Diana stated.

We heard a phone ringing from the other room, and Mike went to find it.

"Hello, Victoria," he said cheerfully. "Fine, how are you? What's up?"

"Not again," Mike said with frustration. "Yes, those are my clients, but I'm not currently working with them. How big of an order? And, she said to send me the bill? Yes, please hold off until I get this settled. I'm so sorry you're having to deal with this."

When Mike disconnected, he explained that Ming had placed a very large order for fabrics with Victoria. Ming had given the names of two of his clients for the job. But she had requested the bill be sent to Mike. It sounded fishy to Victoria, which is why she called. She agreed not to place the order until he got back with her.

"What does that mean?" Diana asked.

"Either Ming is making shit up and trying to stick me with a big bill," Mike explained, "or she's working with my clients and still trying to stick me with the bill."

"Can you call them?" I asked.

"I'm on it," Mike replied as he went upstairs to his office for their contact numbers.

"Ming's not going to stop, is she?" I asked Diana.

"Not until someone stops her," she replied.

A few minutes later, Mike returned and said that both

clients were confused. Neither had talked with Ming or had work they needed done at the moment.

"She's trying to break me," Mike said. "If that order was placed, I'd be responsible for it."

"You couldn't return it?" Diana asked.

"Ming was clever," Mike explained. "If it had been a full bolt, then yes, I probably could have sent it back. But she ordered various patterns cut in lengths that would be considered custom and non-returnable. I'm just grateful Victoria is looking out for me."

"What about your other vendors?" I asked.

"I better make them aware of her scheme and hope it's not too late," Mike said.

"Do you need my help?" I asked. "Diana can take my car, and I'll stay and rent a vehicle when I'm ready to go."

"For that matter, I can rent a car," Diana offered.

"No, you guys get on the road," Mike insisted. "I've got work to do and will keep you posted."

I hated leaving but wasn't sure how much help I could be. We gathered our bags and put them in the car. After a long goodbye, Mike finally told us to get out of there, and we hit the road.

For the first hour, Diana and I talked nonstop, going over the what-ifs, and trying to analyze every possible scenario. Eventually, we just rode in silence, and Diana drifted off for a bit. I was afraid I'd be drowsy, but my mind was racing and obsessing over every little detail. I actually felt buzzed.

"How long have I been asleep?" Diana asked when she woke.

"Around forty minutes."

"Sorry," she apologized. "Do you want me to drive?"

"Thanks, I'm good," I said honestly.

Diana looked at her phone to check messages. After a few minutes, she made a comment.

"She's not trying to hide her crazy anymore."

"Ming?" I asked.

"Yes," she replied. "I was curious and checked her online presence. She has posted some off-the-wall QAnon story about a campfire, being betrayed by the Judases among us, labeled as terrorists, etc. And taking our country back."

"Back from whom? The gays?" I asked. "Aren't the Q followers the ones trying to take it? Take it by force, no less.

And, seriously, no one has taken anything from her – unless it's her dignity and sanity."

"This is pretty much a call to arms," Diana added. "Do you think Connie believes this crap? Thinks there is a gay agenda taking over the world?"

"I don't know her that well, but maybe," I said. "I see educated people who refuse to believe facts. They spout lies as truth. If all of your news is from one source and that source is feeding you bullshit, you eventually believe it. If you hear something that contradicts your beliefs, then it must be wrong."

"She has a few likes on her post," Diana shared. "I wonder if any of these are Mike's clients."

Diana read the names to me, and the only familiar name was Connie.

"And there you have it," I said. "Either Connie believes it or is trying to appease Ming. Either way, it sucks."

"I don't see anything new about Mike's business," Diana added, "but her followers are now over twelve hundred."

"Is Ming the new Messiah?" I asked sarcastically. "I wonder what the average IQ level is of her congregants."

"Should I call Mike?" Diana asked.

"Yes," I said. "He needs to be aware and check to see if the names are people he knows."

Diana called and asked Mike if he had had luck contacting his other vendors. He said he'd reached everyone and informed them that unless they talk with him directly about an order, then don't assume it's from him. Most of the companies were ones Mike had worked with for years and built relationships with his contacts. They were appalled at what had happened to him and said they would be on the lookout. Fortunately, there were no pending orders that Mike hadn't placed and nothing in Ming's name.

Diana read Ming's entire post to him but then said she'd take a screenshot and send it to him. None of the names of the people who posted a thumbs up or a heart in response were familiar. Like us, he was once again dismayed by Connie's actions.

"At least Danny hasn't liked her nonsense," Mike pointed out, "yet."

"He's probably still licking his wounds from his last run-in," I added.

"Bobby called and offered to pick up dinner and bring it by

later," Mike shared. "I guess he took Peggy at her word and plans to babysit me."

"That's good," I said sincerely. "If he offers to stay the night, let him."

Diana gave me a strange look.

"If you don't mind," he replied. "I think I'd feel better having someone there."

After we disconnected, Diana asked if I wouldn't be jealous of Bobby staying with Mike. I reminded her that we weren't married and staying over didn't mean an orgy. Plus it appears that Bobby's tastes have gotten younger as he's gotten older.

"I get together with my ex Bill, from a hundred years ago," I admitted. "It's not sexual. Bobby likes younger, and Bill prefers guys with hairy chests. I may have a lot of hair on top but not as much when you make your way downward."

"That may be more than I needed to know," Diana joked.

"There's something comfortable and familiar with an old love," I added. "Especially if it didn't end badly. Or, like with Bill and me, time softened the painful breakup."

"This is really personal," Diana began, "Is sex that big of a deal at your age?"

I couldn't help but laugh. "Are you asking if I ever get horny?"

"Something like that," she replied.

"Of course," I answered honestly. "But maybe more in my mind than in my nether regions. Truthfully, with some of my meds, I'm slower to respond these days. But the companionship and occasional slam-bam-thank-you-ma'am are nice. It's just not a priority."

"I wondered," Diana said. "I certainly enjoy it but also find I've gotten pickier. I've had bad sex, one-sided sex, and everything in between. I enjoy the rush, the tease, the anticipation. And I enjoy giving pleasure to my partner. But I also expect reciprocation, and some men just want to issue a rain check for later. That doesn't work for me."

"I can't believe we're riding along casually discussing sex," I said.

"I don't have a girlfriend to share with," Diana admitted. "Sure, RA is great, but I don't always feel like I can be brutally honest."

"Did you feel that way with Jim?" I asked as she turned her head toward the window.

"We were getting there," she said softly. "I mean, neither of us held back. I guess what I'm trying to say is: we just didn't have enough time."

"I don't know how much time I have left," I began. "None of us are guaranteed a certain amount. But I will always have time for you."

Still looking out the window, Diana stretched her left arm toward me, and I took my right hand off the steering wheel, placed it in her hand and gave a light squeeze.

After a few minutes of awkward silence, I suggested: "Tell me about the new book."

"I think it's a fascinating story," Diana stated, becoming animated. "It begins with Chris and Julie's childhood – two beautiful kids with blond hair."

Diana shared the tale of their teenage and college years. Chris was Julie's protector, a shadow as well as a competitor. He often seduced Julie's boyfriends, saying they could have the best of both worlds. When Julie married Matt, Chris became his lover, confidant, and eventually his partner-in-crime.

Matt was controlling, and Julie and Chris each wanted his approval. He was unfaithful to both of them and eventually cold and distant to Julie. His affairs often ended badly, and Chris would step in to keep things from escalating to where they'd damage Matt's practice or his marriage. When Matt met Dylan – beautiful underage Dylan – he became obsessed. Until Dylan found the strength to confess everything to Julie and beg for help.

When Jim's first book was released, Julie and Chris were already in prison.

Unfortunately, the book brought Matt and Dylan back together. At that time, Jim didn't know the truth. When the pieces did finally fall into place, Jim realized that he had to set the record right. His apology was this book – his atonement.

"There is so much more to the story, but that gives you an idea," Diana added.

"I can't wait to read it," I said. "Do you think it could become a movie?"

"Actually, I think *Peeper* stands the better chance of being turned into a TV show or movie," Diana replied. "It's more salacious, which would make it more talked about. But I'd be happy for either one or both to do well. That would mean more money for the foundation and, in turn, more good to be done in Jim's name."

"Will you go back to the bureau one day?" I asked.

"Originally, I thought I'd be back by now," Diana admitted. "But the longer I'm away, the less I think about it. Of course, then this thing happens with Mike and leaves me chomping at the bit to have my badge and kick some butt."

"Is the foundation something that could be a full-time job?"

"It has taken much more time than I thought. And Jim did make sure I'd be compensated," she explained. "So, yes, it could be my main employment."

"But, you'd miss the Bureau?" I asked, knowing the answer.

"Yes."

"Do you have plans for dinner?"

"No," Diana answered hesitantly. "What are you thinking?"

"Tattinger's," I replied. "I'm anxious to know how the conversation with Peggy went this morning."

"We could just call her," Diana replied matter-of-factly.

"Do it," I suggested anxiously. "Then we can decide about dinner."

Diana called Peggy and explained that we were still on the road, but curious about her proposal to Dylan and Trevor. And that she was putting her on speakerphone.

"I think it went well," Peggy began. "They had been thinking about it, so it didn't come as a shock."

"Did they give you an answer?" I asked.

"No, but I didn't expect them to," she explained. "It's a big decision. Neither one of them has lived anywhere but Hillmont. They have jobs they enjoy and a nice home without a mortgage. I pulled up Tattinger's website, and it's a whole lot fancier than what Charlie's is, or will be."

"But the restaurant part would be Dylan's to create, experiment with, and make his own," Diana stated. "True?"

"Yes, Maggie and I talked about it, and we are willing to let Dylan do his thing," Peggy revealed. "But that also means it has got to be profitable. This would be like owning a restaurant but with a backup plan."

"And a not-so-silent partner," I added.

"Listen, I want it to succeed," Peggy shared. "I would love to take it easy and let Maggie and Dylan run it. Eventually, put it in Maggie's name. But I don't want to give it to her and have it be a burden struggling to make ends meet. Maggie definitely wants the food service part. But she needs someone experienced to deal with it."

"And Trevor?" Diana asked.

"All I can offer him right now is waiter or bartender," Peggy explained. "When Maggie becomes owner, then maybe Trevor could be the manager. Basically, I'm the owner, Maggie is the manager, Dylan is the chef, and there are assorted bartenders and waitstaff. Oh, and a piano player."

"How did you leave it with them?" Diana asked.

"They said they'd give me an answer by the end of the week," Peggy informed us. "If it's no, I'll be placing a want-ad."

After we hung up, I asked Diana again about dinner. She said yes and called RA to join us.

"I want to see them face to face when we ask about it," Diana said. "If there is hesitation at all, I don't want to talk them into it. Their life is good right now and Dylan is still mourning Jim and Jeff."

"I agree," I replied. "Plus, I'd hate to see them go. I know that's selfish. They're young and have so much life ahead of them."

"You'd see them more than me since your boyfriend is in Bellwood," added Diana. "You'll probably move away, too."

"You could move as well," I suggested.

"In other words, just like all the people moving out of California, those of us from Hillmont will be fleeing to Bellwood?" she joked.

"It's an option."

"True," she said, sounding melancholy. "Nothing lasts forever,"

CHAPTER

Seventeen

I was back in my car around seven to pick up Diana for dinner.

"Long time no see," she greeted me as she got in. "The seat's still warm from the three-hour trip home."

"Funny," I responded sarcastically on the way to pick up RA.

I felt a shiver when I turned into the complex where Roberta Ann and Jim lived. I still remember that night vividly – the barricade – the flashing blue lights.

"Are you going to sell Jim's condo?" I asked Diana. "You said it was part of Jim's assets going toward his foundation."

"I guess I've been waiting on RA," Diana replied. "She wanted to move after that night, but now I think she's able to compartmentalize the horror and prefers to stay where she is."

"Why would that matter in listing his unit?" I asked.

"Because, if she is 100% sure that she's staying, then I might buy Jim's condo," Diana shared, surprising me.

"You could live there?" I asked before thinking.

"Sure," she replied. "I've seen way too many murder scenes. Granted, this one was personal. But because it's personal, I feel a connection to Jim when I'm there. I've spent a lot of hours inside his home dealing with the estate. Sometimes, I sit in his den and talk to him and Jeff as well, since that's where he died. Two deaths in the same home just a few months apart. One peacefully and the other brutally murdered. And if you say I'm crazy, I'll kick your ass."

"I totally get it," I admitted. "After Dean died, I'd find myself talking to him. And more recently, when I visit Dylan and Trevor and see the sofa where Jeff spent so much of his last year, I feel a connection to him."

"You know, this girlfriend thing just might work," Diana said as RA locked her front door and got into the car.

"What have I missed?" Roberta Ann asked while buckling her seatbelt.

Diana and I tag-teamed a condensed version of events. RA was dumbfounded by Ming's post and that Connie had liked it. And she got riled up when we told her about the fabric order that got caught just in time.

"You know that word they used for Karen's ex-friend Tammy Lynn?" she began. "Well, I think it also applies to this psychopathic, unbalanced, unhinged, crazy as a loon, demented, vile, mentally ill, spiteful, bitter, dried-up old fake-named crone."

Diana and I were laughing so hard that I could barely drive.

"I've missed you," I said.

"You've always had a way with words," Diana added.

Once we had settled down, RA asked about the boys and Peggy's offer. We explained that they were interested, but hadn't given her a definite answer. We also shared that we had no intention of pushing them.

"It needs to be their decision," Diana added.

"I agree," RA said. "Hell, maybe we should all move to Bellwood."

Diana and I just looked at each other as I steered my car into the restaurant's parking lot.

"No valet on Tuesday, I guess," Diana observed, changing the subject.

The hostess recognized us since we had become regulars. She greeted us warmly before taking us to a table in Trevor's section.

"What are you smiling about?" RA asked Trevor as he approached our table.

"Just thinking about that Valentine's Day when you guys showed up to check me out," Trevor replied.

"Check you out?" Diana repeated. "You're awfully full of yourself, young man."

"Don't listen to her," RA said. "I'm still checking you out."

"What are your specials tonight?" I asked.

"He's not special enough?" Roberta Ann asked.

"Behave," I scolded.

"Someone's feeling feisty," Trevor added before reciting the list of nightly offerings.

Once our drink orders arrived and our dinner orders were taken, I asked if Dylan could slip away and join us. Trevor excused himself and returned shortly, with Dylan following. After the niceties were out of the way, I said:

"Rumor has it you received an offer this morning."

"Definitely no secrets within this group," he replied.

"What did you hear?" Trevor asked, looking around for eavesdroppers. I explained.

"That's pretty much the gist of it," Dylan added. "It's a big decision, but we're interested."

"We just need to sleep on it a day or two," Trevor shared.

"What about Mike?" Dylan asked. "Have things settled down?"

"Not really, but it's too long to get into it while you're working," I answered.

"Have you seen the book yet?" Dylan asked Diana.

"No, we just got home a couple of hours ago," she explained. "But I'm meeting with the lawyer in the morning and will let you know."

"From what Diana has told me, you're going to be pleased," I added for encouragement.

"I better get back to work," Dylan remarked. "Your dinners aren't going to cook themselves."

"Anyone need another drink?" Trevor asked as Dylan walked away. He then whispered: "He wants to do it but is concerned about me – wanting to make sure I'll be happy. I told him as long as we're together, I'm happy."

RA took an audible breath as tears formed in her eyes.

Trevor, realizing she was getting emotional, kissed her cheek and walked away.

"Damn, he is beyond precious," RA said. "Imagine being that much in love."

"I don't think that I ever was," I admitted.

"Same here," Diana added.

"Peggy just sent a text asking if I've heard anything," I shared. "What do I say?"

"Tell her all you know is that they're considering it and will let her know something in a few days," Diana instructed. "You don't want to encourage her in case they change their minds."

Our dinners were perfection as always. Diana brought up something that I hadn't thought about. Peggy and Maggie are so hot-to-trot to get Dylan to be their chef, yet they've never tasted his food or seen his presentations. If he did for Charlie's just half of what he had done for Tattinger's, word would get out, and it wouldn't be only the gays flocking there.

"Do you have any sales coming up?" I asked Roberta Ann. "You used to have something everything weekend."

"I still do," she replied. "But I don't have to work them. I promoted one gal who now handles most of the average sales. I step in on the high-ticket ones, – or for people I know. This way, I get to take a little time for myself."

"That's wonderful," Diana said approvingly.

"I may make a little less money by paying her more," RA added. "But my sanity has got to be worth something. I've been doing this for twenty-plus years."

"And what about your condo?" I asked. "Diana said at one time you had considered selling."

"I did at first," RA explained. "I was having nightmares and thought I needed a change. I'd see Jim everywhere I looked. And then, it almost became a comfort. I'm dreading the idea of a new neighbor. But, I know it will eventually have to be sold."

Diana looked at me and glared.

"I told Ricky something today, and I think he's trying to 'out' me," Diana began.

"You're a lesbian?" RA said a little too loudly.

"No, and lower your voice," she scolded.

"I'm considering buying Jim's condo for myself," she revealed. "I just wanted to make sure you weren't going anywhere and that you'd be okay with it."

"Are you kidding me?" RA asked. "That would be the next best thing to having Jim there. Sorry, I didn't mean it the way it sounded."

"It sounded perfectly fine," Diana replied. "I couldn't think of anything better than to have Jim still there – still with us."

"Are you guys okay?" asked Trevor. "You look like you're about to cry."

Since neither of the girls could talk, I stepped in.

"It appears that Diana is going to buy Jim's condo and move in next door to RA," I explained.

"What a perfect solution," Trevor exclaimed. "I had said something to Dylan about us buying it, but he told me there was no way he could live there. He also said that he couldn't imagine some stranger living there either."

"Diana may be strange, but at least she's not a stranger," I inserted into the conversation.

"You are such a turd," she responded, laughing.

"So, we both may have a move in our future," Trevor added.

Just then, Dylan walked over carrying a tray with three lavish desserts. Trevor placed one in front of each of us and then asked if we'd like some freshly brewed decaf.

"By the way," he said to Dylan, "you just missed the big announcement. Diana is going to buy Jim's condo."

Dylan then said something that made our hearts burst with joy. "You mean it's going to stay in the family?" he asked.

"I had never thought of it that way," Diana said. "But yes, it stays in the family."

Roberta Ann commented on the way home that a delicious meal with wonderful friends, along with knowing Diana would soon be next door and Jim's spirit would live on, had made her happier than she had been in a long, long time.

—●—

For the next few days, things appeared to have died down in Bellwood. Nothing out of Ming, Connie or Danny. Ming hadn't posted anything off the wall, and her recent QAnon post had been taken down. Mike didn't know anything more about the client Ming had stolen other than Victoria saying the fabric had been shipped and that Ming should have it by now.

I wanted to believe it was over. But that's rarely the case. While we were having lunch a few days later, Diana was notified by her Bellwood contact that Ming had been arrested for trespassing. We were floored to learn it was Peggy who had called the police.

"What happened?" Diana yelled when Peggy answered. "Why didn't you call me?"

"Calm down," Peggy said on speaker. "I saw someone in my backyard – a woman in a sweatshirt with a hood and sunglasses. I had never met Ming and didn't even see her when she was in my house. But this woman was wearing animal print leggings, and let me just say, she had no business wearing anything that tight! I wondered if it was her. I called the cops just as she tried my backdoor, checking to see if it was locked. An officer was in the area and snagged her."

"You should have let me know," Diana said.

"And what could you have done from Hillmont other than worry?" Peggy asked. "I didn't want to upset you when you've got so much more to do than worry about me."

"You're my friend, Peggy. Us alphas have got to look out for each other," Diana said, surprising herself. "And I do worry."

I just looked at her and smiled. And, in typical Diana fashion, she stuck out her tongue.

"I heard she said she was your interior designer and was just getting measurements," Diana continued.

"Yeah, but the dumb broad didn't even have a tape measure on her," Peggy explained. "I think they just gave her a ticket or a warning. Again, it wasn't serious enough to lock her away."

"So, you're okay?" Diana asked.

"Yes, but Mike's having a meltdown," Peggy replied. "He thinks it's his fault."

"If it's anyone's fault, it's mine for having her come to your house in the first place," Diana said. "I'm the one who exposed you."

"You think I haven't dealt with crazies before?" Peggy asked. "I own a damn gay bar, for heaven's sake. Speaking of drama!"

Diana and I both began to laugh. Nothing was going to faze Peggy.

"When are you coming back, Ricky?" Peggy asked. "We've got a bar to remodel."

"When are you holding your auditions?" I asked, changing the subject.

"Next week. And get this – Victor said we could do it at the piano store," Peggy shared. "Maggie thinks he wants to size up the competition. We've got leads on three different guys. No girls, so Val will be pissed."

"You better call me at the next sign of trouble," Diana said sternly.

"Damn, you're bossy," Peggy replied.

"Right back at ya, girlfriend," Diana added, laughing.

It was my turn to scold, so I called Mike.

"Ming was caught trespassing on Peggy's property, and we have to hear about it from the local cops?" I began. "You didn't think we'd want to know about it?"

"What would you do other than worry?" he replied.

"Did you and Peggy coordinate responses?" I asked. "That's what she told Diana."

"I'm just furious at myself for involving her," Mike added.

"Don't even say it's your fault," I snapped. "It's that crazy mad hatter friend of yours fault."

"Could you narrow it down a bit? I have several who qualify – you included," Mike joked.

"Feeling kind of cocky, are you? Before you say anything off-color, let me remind you that Diana is sitting here with me."

"Hey, D," Mike said. "I wouldn't want to upset your delicate sensibilities."

"FU," was Diana's curt response.

"In all seriousness, when do you think you'll be back?" Mike asked. "I'd hoped Dylan and Trevor would have said yes by now. Regardless, I could use Dylan's help."

"Whatcha need?" I asked.

"We have the layout for the kitchen, but I don't know which brands he prefers for the additional equipment. I need to price it out and see what's in stock."

"I'll call him when we hang up and get back with you," I replied. "Is everything else we talked about available?"

"Yes," he replied. "Oh, and by the way, Peggy must not have told you that they're auditioning two guys Monday and another the next day for the piano player job. There was one more, but he's already bowed out."

"Sounds like fun," Diana said.

"Let me get hold of Dylan and see what I can find out," I offered. "Hopefully, I can call you back in a minute."

When Dylan answered, I posed my question as if he had already said yes. So what would be his top choices be for "his" kitchen at Charlie's?

"I've been waiting for you to ask," Dylan replied. "I've made a list that I can send to you with my first and second choices. Something may not be within budget or could be backordered indefinitely, so I wanted to give you options. And, yes, we have made our decision."

"You have?" I asked excitedly. "What did you decide?"

"I haven't told Peggy and Maggie yet – and let's be honest here, you couldn't keep a secret if your life depended on it," Dylan, said laughing. "Let me call them, and then I'll call you back."

"You're wrong about the secret-keeping," I said with attitude. "I kept the Nathaniel and the Midnight Movers' adventures a secret for more years than you've been alive."

"Fine. Our answer is yes, and it better not get back to me before I've told Peggy," Dylan warned. "That's not a great way for me to start a business relationship."

"I agree, and your secret is safe with me," I promised. "For now!"

"Damn, I better call Peggy immediately before you give it away," Dylan said, disconnecting.

I waited for him to send me the list but figured he had to make his call to Peggy first. I wanted to be excited and happy for them, but there was a sadness attached to it, knowing they'd be moving away. After about ten minutes, Dylan called back to say it was done and that the list was on its way. They also planned on going to Bellwood Sunday and Monday and wondered if they could stay with Mike.

"Of course, you can," I replied. "We can ride together if you'd like."

"We'll need to be back Tuesday morning for work that evening," Dylan explained. "And I bet you'll be staying longer."

"That's probably true," I admitted.

I called Mike, but Peggy had beaten me to the punch. I said I had a list of options for the kitchen and would forward it to him. He was elated to have the boys stay with him and offered to call Val so she could get her realtor friend lined up. That reminded me that I hadn't asked Dylan what he planned to do with Jeff's house. In the current market, where homes were getting offers over the asking price, selling felt like the right thing. Most of the furnishings had been Jeff's, and I wasn't sure if they'd move them to Bellwood or want to start fresh. Regardless, RA could help them with a sale.

Diana, like me, had mixed emotions when I gave her the news. She added that she'd like to ride over with me but then ride back with the boys.

"I need a couple of days to follow up on some things in Bellwood, and then I want to get back and make arrangements for my own move."

CHAPTER
Eighteen

Saturday was uneventful, and that was a welcome change. Diana began packing things that she didn't need on a daily basis. After her divorce, she rented an apartment for several years. It was nice but generic. She had looked at it as a temporary fix. Jim's condo would be something that she could make her own. I asked her about his furnishings, and she said she might keep a few things and then ask RA to sell the rest. Roberta Ann still had a warehouse where she could hold sales offsite. Since Jim's condo would be a magnet for curiosity seekers, they decided they'd move the pieces to the warehouse for her sale.

I paid bills, washed clothes, and changed the linens on my bed. Next, I packed a suitcase since I had planned to stay for several days. That evening I tried to watch TV but was unable to focus. Mike and I had toyed with the idea of moving in together, but we both knew it wasn't going to happen. However, with Dylan and Trevor planning to move to Bellwood, I wondered if maybe I should think more seriously about it.

I certainly wasn't getting any younger, and I was not excited at the prospect of growing old alone. Bill, my ex and friend of more than forty years, still lived in Hillmont, and we'd get together every two to three weeks. But our conversations were usually rooted in the past. And as much as I loved Diana and RA, they were young enough to be my daughters. The friends my age – Mike, Bobby, Val, Char and Karen – all lived in Bellwood. Gayle and Connie also fit the bill, but did they consider me their friend? Or was I Mike's friend who they tolerated? Peggy was a few years older, but we had a connection because of Dean.

I couldn't see Mike and me living together. We enjoyed our time alone too much. Plus, there was no room for me in his home, and I was doubtful he'd want to move. Still, I could have my own place, and we could be together as much as we wanted to. What's that song by K.T. Oslin? *Live Close By and Visit Often?* I thought that would be the best solution.

—•—

Diana and I got an early start the next morning and arrived in Bellwood a little after ten. We had not eaten and were grateful that Mike had picked up bagels, cream cheese, fruit and had coffee ready.

"I gather that you haven't had any Ming sightings recently?" Diana asked him. "Maybe that trespass warning convinced her to lay low."

"I don't think we've heard the last of her," Mike said. "I want her out of my life, but I don't see it happening quite yet."

"Did you ever talk with your client who hired Ming?" I asked. "You've only gotten Ming's side of the story."

"She was so evasive when I called about the Ming's email," Mike began, "that I doubt she'd talk with me now."

"What if I called her in an official, non-official capacity?" Diana suggested. "Just a few friendly questions since Ming has committed several offenses lately."

"I'd love to know what she has to say," I added. "That is, if it won't get you into trouble."

"I'll have to be careful how I word things," Diana admitted. "But I think I can pull it off."

"Let me get you her number," Mike offered.

Mike's former client, Frieda, answered on the third ring. Diana introduced herself as being "out of" the Hillmont office of the State Bureau of Investigations. She explained that she was "gathering information" on Ming Leatherwood and understood that Frieda had hired her in an interior design capacity.

"Is that correct?" Diana asked.

Frieda replied that she had initially talked with Ming but had decided to put everything on hold for now. She was also curious why Ming was under investigation.

"I can't really reveal that now. There have been complaints," Diana explained. "May I ask why you decided to postpone having work done?"

"If I can be honest?" Frieda asked her. "She scares me. The things that she said about Mike were unprofessional. And, I don't know if you're aware, but I've seen her online posts making fun of COVID, the vaccine, and supporting QAnon."

"You disagree with her politically?" Diana asked.

"I'm a Republican, but I'm not one of the crazy ones,"

Frieda replied. "I asked if she was vaccinated, and she said she didn't believe in it. She told me that God would protect her. Well, I believe in God, but I also believe he gave us brains to help ourselves, and the ability to create these vaccines for protection. I don't expect God to protect me if I'm foolish enough to have people like her in my home."

"Were you aware of Ms. Leatherwood doing anything illegal?" Diana asked, and Frieda answered no.

She then thanked her for her time and ended the call.

"It sounds like this Frieda lady didn't believe Ming's lies, found her unstable, and dangerous when it comes to COVID," I surmised.

"That makes me feel a little better," Mike said. "And it sounds like Ming is stuck with that fabric order Victoria said has arrived."

"Any word on Gayle?" Diana asked.

"She's better," Mike shared. "Karen did ask her if Connie had been in touch, and she said no. She was as confused as the rest of us that Ming introduced Connie as her associate at Peggy's. She has no idea why Connie was there in the first place."

It was after twelve when Dylan and Trevor arrived. They put their things in the room they had stayed in last weekend. And Diana made herself at home in the other guest room.

The boys had eaten on the road and planned to meet Peggy at two. They needed to finalize their work agreement and wanted to look everything over again now that a decision had been made. Mike and I waited until four to run by the bar.

"Diana has already made the funds available, so I'm ready as soon as you are," Peggy shared. "What I need from you is a starting date to announce when we'll be closed. And, if possible, a comfortable date for reopening."

"Right now, I'm thinking that you can go through next weekend with the work beginning one week from tomorrow," Mike explained. "As far as reopening, if nothing unforeseen happens, you could reopen by the end of the month."

"I think the grand reopening should be on a Saturday," Peggy suggested.

"The only kink in our plan would be the inspections," Mike admitted. "I don't know how backed up they might be. I wish we had a contact person in that department."

"Maybe I should leave the reopening date as more of a stay tuned date, so we don't get caught needing to reschedule," Peggy suggested.

"Will Dylan be ready by then?" I asked.

"They'll give their two-week notice to Tattinger's tomorrow," Peggy explained. "That would work out fine and give them time to move as well as get the kitchen set up."

"Even if they find a home, they won't be able to close on it that quickly," Mike said.

"They've thought of that and plan to do a short-term lease on an apartment," Peggy explained. "They said they will need to close the sale of their home to be able to purchase a new one."

"And Dylan thinks he'll have the kitchen in order and a menu decided in time?" I asked.

"He already knows some of the dishes he'd like to offer," Peggy replied. "But he suggested, and I agreed, that we won't open with a full dinner menu. We'll tease that it's coming, along with a Sunday brunch option. His idea is to begin with an expanded appetizer and small plates menu that can be shared."

"That sounds like a perfect solution," I said. "I'm impressed that he came up with the idea. You certainly don't want to be unprepared and unable to provide what you offer. As you know, you only have one chance to make a great impression."

"By the way," Peggy began, "no one thought of china and flatware. Don't worry, Maggie and I went by the restaurant supply place and found what we needed."

"I'm sure it will be fine," Mike said, and I agreed.

We asked Peggy about the pianist auditions, and she explained that Victor and another guy would have their audition tomorrow, with a third guy on Tuesday. When she asked about having the piano delivered, we suggested that she wait until the last minute. We didn't want it to be in the way of the workers and possibly get damaged. We wanted to make sure that construction dust was long gone.

"If we're all set, then I'll put out a sign and have Maggie post on social media the closure and the announcement of what's coming soon," Peggy stated. "I'm excited and nervous as hell."

—•—

The five of us were back at Charlie's that evening around eight. Karen and Bobby had already arrived and were seated at our makeshift banquet table. Val and Char showed up about five minutes later. Once we had our drinks, Peggy announced that she needed to bring everyone up to speed.

"First, what about Gayle?" she asked.

"I talked with her earlier, and she sounded much better," Karen shared. "Luckily, no one else in her family caught it. She said she'll retest in a few days and check with her doctor to see if she thinks she's ready to get out of quarantine."

"That's good news," Char said. "We have three friends right now in the same situation. All have been vaccinated and had the booster, and they say their symptoms are mild."

"You have to wonder how long we're going to be dealing with this," Bobby said. "How many times will it mutate into something else?"

"As long as there are people like Ming out there, ignoring science and not concerned for others, then I'm not sure it will ever be gone," added Val.

"Speaking of which," Maggie began, "any news on Ming and Connie?"

"I'm not aware of anything regarding Connie," Diana shared. "The one-on-one with me at Peggy's house may have scared her enough to rethink her relationship with Ming. I checked with my local sources today, and Ming has managed to stay off their radar after getting caught trespassing at Peggy's. A new concern popped up – although it may be nothing."

"I don't like the sound of that," Peggy said.

"Ming's posts are one thing, but it's her followers' comments that make me uneasy," Diana explained. "I've noticed several times Ming responds saying she'll send them a private message or text."

"And, what bothers you is that we can't see her message?" Karen asked.

"Right," Diana confirmed.

"I haven't seen any crazy-ass posts recently," Val stated, scrolling through her phone. "Oh shit, wait. She posted this a couple of hours ago."

Val read, as we all searched for Ming's page, the announcement for a Celebration of Life service for Gator one week from this Sunday at two pm at the Long Valley Funeral Home's chapel.

"We've got to go," Bobby said. "It is bound to be a train wreck of the first degree."

"Why the funeral home, I wonder?" Val commented. "I thought Gator was cremated a while back."

"I've never known Ming to have any affiliation with a church," Mike added. "If the funeral home did the cremation, then maybe holding a service there was an option."

"Those inbox messages you were concerned about could be personal invitations to the memorial service," Char added.

"I just pulled up the funeral home's website out of curiosity," Maggie said. "I noticed that Ming's announcement didn't have the usual COVID restrictions disclaimer that we've come to expect. However, the funeral home does say masks are required."

"I'm surprised Ming would go along with that," I added. "Especially since she has been vehemently opposed to any precautions."

"I agree with Bobby," Val said. "We have to go."

"I wonder if Connie will be there," Mike commented.

"I'd think that would be a given from what we've already seen," Peggy explained.

"I just sent Gayle a text to let her know," Karen shared. "She said as long as she tests negative, she'll plan on joining us."

"Do you think any of your design clients will come?" Dylan asked.

"Or Danny?" Trevor added.

"This should be interesting," Diana stated. "I'll see if one of my contacts might accompany me, just in case things get out of hand."

"Enough about Ming," Peggy announced. "That woman has consumed too much of our lives already. Let me tell you about Charlie's."

For the next thirty minutes, Peggy, Maggie, Dylan, Trevor, Mike and I discussed the future of Charlie's. Mike and I described what would happen with the renovation – how long it "should" take – and when we hoped we could finish. Dylan talked about his ideas for the restaurant and the different stages that would occur until it had fully reached his dream. We all agreed that it was wise to start off small with limited options to allow Dylan to become comfortable with the kitchen. Plus, he would need to get a feel for what the clientele wanted. Maggie explained the audition process to find a pianist/entertainer.

"Right now, the only unknown is the inspection process,"

Mike said. "Sometimes that can take weeks to get an inspector to sign off on everything."

"That sucks," Bobby commented.

"Next Sunday will be the last day for Charlie's as you see it now," Peggy said with a twinge of emotion.

There were many questions and much excitement as we discussed the changes. Then, Val asked Trevor and Dylan to tell us about their appointment with the realtor."

"First of all, she's great," Trevor said. "Thank you for the introduction."

"Obviously, we can't have our home sold and be closed in time to buy something here and have it closed as well as moved in before the opening," Dylan explained. "We'll go ahead and list our home in Hillmont. I feel certain that it will sell quickly."

"And thank you to Jeff for making this possible for us," Trevor said as Diana raised her glass to toast our old friend.

"Tomorrow, we're going to look at several condominiums," Dylan continued. "Trevor and I have decided we're not ready for the upkeep of a house and yard, as busy as we plan to be with Charlie's."

"If we do find something, we feel confident we can go ahead and make an offer," Trevor added. "We have the earnest money and possibly the down payment, even without the sale of Dylan's home."

"*Our* home," Dylan corrected Trevor. "Ideally, we'll get it sold and be able to pay cash for whatever we find here."

"Again, thanks to Jeff's generosity," Trevor added.

"I don't know how much we'll bring with us," Dylan said. "Jeff's taste is not our taste. And yet, I know I want to keep a few of his things as a reminder. He will always be a part of our lives."

"We've already asked RA about having a sale for us," Trevor shared. "Maybe in conjunction with Diana's sale."

"You're having a sale?" Karen asked.

"I'm buying my friend Jim's condo," Diana replied. "Like the boys, I want to keep some of Jim's furnishings as a reminder. Roberta Ann will find new homes for the rest."

"Ricky," Bobby asked, "will you be having a sale soon, or do you plan on moving everything to Bellwood?"

"I haven't said I'm moving," I quickly answered as Diana and Mike looked questioningly at me.

"I think that you should," Diana said.

"But..." I began.

"I'll be okay," she said. "I'll have RA right next door, and you'll always have a place to stay when you visit."

"Mike," I began, "you know we can't live together. We're too old and set in our ways. And, bottom line, you don't have any room."

"I know," he admitted. "But, you could live close by and visit often."

Those words felt like a sign from above. I knew I'd be a fool if I ignored them.

"Val," I said. "You think you could introduce me to your realtor?"

CHAPTER

Nineteen

The next day was a whirlwind, with so many things happening at the same time. Dylan and Trevor met with the realtor and looked at five different condos. It was the fifth one that got their juices flowing. They explained later that the others were very nice but, one complex appeared to have a much older demographic – quickly adding that they meant no offense. And the other three units were in the same complex that appeared to be inundated with children.

"The one we chose is downtown in a converted warehouse," Dylan said. "It has high ceilings, brick walls, and windows overlooking the river."

"Most of the owners range in age from their twenties to their forties," Trevor explained. "And, they have planned monthly social activities – not that our schedules will permit. But, it's nice to know there are options."

"This unit is on the third floor, which is the top floor," Dylan shared. "It has two bedrooms, two baths, and a second-floor loft overlooking the great room. The best part is a secured parking garage with two assigned spaces."

"The owner has already moved out, so we proposed renting it until our home sells and we're able to close on it," Trevor added excitedly. "We're hoping they'll accept our offer."

"Judging on what Jeff's house should bring," Dylan continued, "we should be able to buy this and not have a mortgage."

"That's incredible," Diana said. "Ricky, maybe you should look at the complex they said had all the old farts. You'd fit right in!"

"You're not as funny as you think you are," I replied as Diana smiled.

"Jim also said that to me once," she shared.

—•—

Peggy called later to update us on the audition process. Once again, I put her on speaker so we could all hear.

"Victor was the better of the two," she said. "Bobby may just have to get over it. He can read music as well as play by ear. We had a few song titles in mind, and when we threw them at him, he had no problem playing them. Plus, he's personable, cute and not in a relationship. So, hopefully, no drama."

"What about the other one?" I asked.

"No dice," Peggy said bluntly. "Oh, he can play the piano. Very talented. But, I threw out a Dolly song, then Garth, and one by George Strait. He was clueless and said he never listens to country music and was not familiar with our requests. However, he did say that he'd heard Dolly's '9 to 5' before."

"Uh, oh," Mike commented. "You've got to know Dolly's song catalog if you're going to make it at Charlie's."

"Damn, straight," Peggy snapped. "We'll wait to see about the guy who's auditioning tomorrow, but for now, Victor's the one. Should I tell the others?"

"You might as well wait until you've heard the next guy and made a final decision," Dylan suggested.

"Sounds good," Peggy responded.

The next day Diana and the boys left early to drive back to Hillmont. She had received notice that the shipment of

Jim's second book would arrive today. Dylan and Trevor needed to be at work by three. They had emailed their resignation notice to the restaurant's owner yesterday and were nervous to see him face to face. I asked one of them to text me to let me know if everything went okay. That afternoon Trevor shared that the owner had suspected Dylan would leave one day and that Trevor would join him. He handled it well and wished them the best. You couldn't ask for a better response.

"I think the fact that we were moving away instead of going to a local competitor helped," Trevor added.

—●—

"It's Victor," Peggy announced when I answered the phone.

"I take it the audition didn't go well," I said.

"This one could play, too. But only if the sheet music was in front of him," Peggy shared. "He arrived with a suitcase of music books. When we made a request, he would start sorting through them to find the song. I swear it would take five minutes of searching to play a three-minute song."

"Sounds comical and annoying," I remarked.

"Exactly," she confirmed.

Diana called later to share that the books had arrived and that she was so proud of the way it had turned out – adding that she would overnight a copy to me. When it showed up the next day, I sat on the porch and read straight through. Even though I knew so much of the story, seeing it told in chronological order with many of the blanks filled in made for an emotional read. Mike had appointments and errands to do, giving me the house to myself. Other than setting a time to meet with the realtor tomorrow, I stayed immersed in *Redemption* until the end.

"I didn't want to interrupt you when I got home, so I went upstairs and got caught up on invoices," Mike explained when I walked back into the house. "How was it?"

"Draining," I explained. "but in a good way. I think it's a powerful read for anyone. But as someone who knew the players, I felt completely engrossed in the story. Almost as if it were happening in real-time and I was there. I don't know how else to describe it. We were all so wrong about Julie and Chris and what they went through. Reading about Dylan and how he got caught up in their world broke my heart."

"May I read it?" Mike asked. "I need to be immersed in something other than Ming and Connie. I know I have to be there Sunday at the service, but I fear it will only make things worse."

"Or, you might finally get closure," I suggested.

Mike began the book after dinner and didn't come to bed until after I had fallen asleep. The next morning he said that he couldn't put it down. He had never met Julie, Chris or Matt but had formed an opinion from what I had shared. However, he did know Dylan and Jim, which made it personal for him.

"I wish Jim could have been the one to release this," Mike said. "Diana did a great job, but this is Jim's story."

The rest of the week was devoted to making sure everything was in order to begin the Charlie's project. Lighting, tables, chairs, and kitchen fixtures were waiting to be delivered. The carpenters would begin first thing Monday expanding the kitchen. The painters would start at the opposite end of the space, working toward the new wall giving time for the construction dust to settle. All of the booths would be pulled out for painting, then turned and reconfigured once the paint had dried. Since the kitchen had a back door to the employee parking area, the workers could access it from there and not track through the refreshed bar area.

—•—

Diana and the boys arrived in Bellwood at noon on Sunday to attend the circus that would be Gator's Celebration of Life service. Mike had ordered sandwiches, slaw, potato salad and sweets and asked everyone to stop by. That way, we could all leave together and arrive at the funeral home at the same time.

Gayle had been given a clean bill of health and rode with Bobby and Karen. Peggy and Maggie had their own cars, as did Val and Char. Everyone was speculating on what might happen. Diana had convinced one of the guys from the Bureau office to meet her there. He came more out of curiosity than thinking there would be trouble.

At one-thirty, we divided up into four cars and drove to the funeral home. Mike and Peggy said they only recognized a couple of people going in. The parking lot was nearly full, which surprised me. But, as Mike pointed out, Ming and Gator were Bellwood natives and had connections outside of their work.

"And none of us knows how many might be here because of Ming's online presence," Diana reminded us.

Once we were all assembled and had our masks on, Peggy said, "Stick together and don't leave a man behind."

"Or woman," Val added as Char rolled her eyes.

The chapel had shiny gold ornate mirrors equally spaced down the side walls. The pews were painted white and covered in red velvet, matching the wall-to-wall carpet. An over-the-top crystal chandelier hung dead center from the vaulted ceiling. A raised platform had four throne-like chairs and a podium painted to match the pews. An easel off to the side held an oversized photograph of Gator and Ming in wedding attire. There were smaller framed photos on a table beside it.

Ming, wearing a low-cut animal print t-shirt and painted-on black jeans, sat in a chair to the left of the podium without a mask. Two men, one with and one without a mask, occupied the chairs to the right.

We sat in two rows near the middle as the front pews and the back rows were already filled. Diana saw her friend in law enforcement and motioned for him to join her. He was young and buff, with neatly trimmed sandy brown hair. Bobby looked him over from head to toe.

Connie was sitting near the front with a younger woman – almost her clone. Their blonde hair glowed under the light from the gaudy chandelier. Gayle whispered that she was Connie's daughter, Sara, adding that she didn't understand why Connie had brought her.

Once the recorded organ music had stopped, one of the men stepped up to the podium, removed his mask, and introduced himself. He explained that he worked for Long Valley Funeral Home, and thanked everyone for being there. He also encouraged us to wear our masks to protect ourselves and our neighbors. Then he talked about what a loss it was and how he had come to know Gator and Ming when they renovated the funeral home with new window treatments.

"So, that's the connection," Mike whispered.

Surprisingly, he added that they had suffered their share of COVID-related illnesses and deaths in the Long Valley family. And, he said that you can never be too careful.

"Sadly, this is our fourth funeral service for one of our own due to COVID," the funeral director shared. "We're not through with this awful plague. All we can do is be careful and get vaccinated."

"Oh, my God," I said. "If that doesn't tick Ming off, nothing will."

He then introduced the maskless man as a friend of the family. The "friend" stepped forward and spoke about growing up with Gator. He talked about what a good man he was – describing him as gentle, kind, and funny. He then shared that Ming had been Gator's one true love, and that she had saved him from a loveless marriage.

"Talk about bad taste," Karen said. "What an awful thing to say."

"Is his son here?" I asked. No one seemed to know.

"Ming's a good woman trying to do the best she can," the friend continued. "I know there are some who have tried to beat her down with their lies. People she had worked with and felt close to have now turned on her."

I took Mike's hand in mine.

"But she is strong and will overcome their hate," he added. "They will see that they were wrong, and they will have to pay on judgment day."

"Shit," Val said a little too loudly.

"I advised her against this, but Ming feels the need to speak here today," her friend explained. "Despite of all of the pain she has endured, she wants to speak up for Gator."

Diana looked over at me, and although I could only see her eyes above the mask, I could hear her channeling Bette Davis and warning us to fasten our seat belts for a bumpy night.

Ming stood and – I swear to God – adjusted her bosom, stepping forward. She took a long hard look at those of us in attendance before she began speaking.

"She's way too old to be wearing that outfit," Peggy said under her breath.

"Thank you for being here," Ming began. "Although I'm surprised that some of you had the balls to show up."

Nervous laughter rumbled through the chapel as some shifted in their seats.

"My Gator was a good man," she said. "Some have tried to say otherwise, but they're wrong. When I met him, he was miserable. You may think I broke up his marriage, but it was already over, and he was looking for a way to escape. But, he was tied down by a kid who he wasn't even sure was his."

"Damn!" someone uttered behind us.

"I threw him a life jacket and gave him a reason to continue living," Ming shared. "We had an amazing marriage, and don't you think otherwise. He loved me, worshipped me, and I had him wrapped around my little finger. That's what mind-blowing sex can do to a man."

The funeral director shifted in his chair, and Gator's friend smiled and nodded in agreement. This was becoming more uncomfortable by the minute.

"Gator didn't get the vaccination because he knew it's a government-controlled hoax," she stated. "All of you who did are just sheep. It wasn't even COVID that killed him. His heart was just too full and finally gave out."

"She's rewriting history," Mike was getting increasingly agitated. "I have texts she wrote admitting that they both had caught it."

"I know," I said calmly. "But, this is not the time or place."

Diana looked concerned about Mike, and I couldn't blame her. I prayed that he'd keep it together.

"Gator loved me so much that, well, you know what he told me before taking his last breath?" she asked. "He confessed that there was one time many years ago that he had cheated on me. Can you imagine a man ever cheating on me? Anyway, it wasn't his fault."

"Where is she going with this?" Peggy asked.

"You see, that rotten boy of his was always causing trouble," Ming continued. "Always needing money or something from his daddy. Well, this time, he came to the house with some sleazy new girlfriend. And this girl realized that my Gator would be a much better catch than his worthless son. While I'm cooking dinner and the boy runs back to the store for beer, this bimbo makes her move on my man."

Just then, Connie's daughter, Sara, stood and rushed out of the room.

"No, it can't be," Gayle said, horrified.

"And there she goes now!" Ming added, pointing to Sara. Then, turning to point at Connie, she said: "And there's the sorry mother who raised her daughter to be a whore. See, I didn't know about it back then. They all kept it a secret from me. Funny thing is, I met the mother many years later. Still, I didn't know the connection. And I didn't know what had happened that night until Gator took his last breath."

Gayle got up, walked to the front and sat next to Connie. I couldn't understand why Connie didn't leave to check on her daughter.

Every head turned to watch Gayle take her seat next to Connie.

"Oh look, Mother-of-the-Year has a friend," Ming remarked. "Anyway, Gator told me about that night when he showed his son's date my workroom. How she made a move on him, and he tried to stop her. But the devil was stronger, and he finally gave in to that temptress. Gator told me that no one knew about it – except for Mike, a man who pretended to be our friend. He's sitting back there with the other queers and lesbos."

Some of the mourners began to boo, turning in their seats to find us.

"Let's leave," I said.

"No," Mike replied. "I'm going to see it through."

Diana whispered something to her Bureau companion. And Peggy said, "Be strong."

"This guy we had worked with for years, who we considered a close friend, knew about my husband's infidelities and never thought to tell me," Ming, looking wild-eyed, was ranting now.

"I found Gator's kid and asked him about it. He didn't know what I was talking about, and trust me, he's too dumb to lie. I asked him who that girl was. Well, it had been a long time, but he came up a name. Said they only went out that one time."

The crowd was getting restless and louder, yet no one got up to leave.

"The girl's last name was familiar. I had a design job a few years back with someone who had the same last name. I wondered if there was a connection," Ming explained. "I made up an excuse to contact the client and eventually found out that she did have a daughter by that name, although the girl's now married with a kid of her own. I told her about her tramp of a daughter and what she did to my Gator."

"Oh, no," Karen said. "Poor Connie."

"Of course, she denied it. Said I had to be mistaken," Ming continued, sounding more and more like a revival-tent preacher. "But, I told her to ask her daughter if it was true. I said I'd call back the next day."

"When I called back, Connie – that's her name – said it was Gator who had attacked her daughter. I asked her, then why didn't her girl report it? Why didn't she call the cops? And she tells me her daughter didn't want anyone to know. But I know why. She knew Gator would tell the cops the truth. Tell them how *she* seduced him."

"This is worse than I could have imagined," Bobby whispered loudly.

"Does she really believe what she's saying?" Val asked.

"And, get this – Connie begs me not to tell anyone. Says she'll do anything to keep it a secret. Anything to protect her daughter's reputation," Ming adds, laughing sadistically. "Well, I guess she didn't do enough, did she? Now all of you know what her girl did to my husband."

The room had become eerily quiet. No one moved. No one said a thing. It was as if time stood still. And then a woman near the back stood and began to clap. She kept applauding as she stepped into the aisle and walked forward.

"What a crock of shit, Dottie Mae," she began. "That *is* your real name, isn't it? Dottie Mae Derryberry? I saw your picture in my mom's high school yearbook. By the way, Ann was her name. You called her Poke Salad Annie after a song that came out that year. I heard you loved to make fun of her. You knew her, and you knew what happened to her."

"Who are you, and what do you want?" Ming defiantly asked.

"You know exactly who I am," she replied, turning to face the crowd. "For the rest of you here today, my name is Delores Payne. Several of you know me from teaching your children at Westside Elementary.

Everyone was hanging onto Delores' every word.

"On the day my mother turned seventeen, Luther, who most of you know as Gator, raped and assaulted her."

"That's a lie!" Ming screamed.

"No, it's not," Dolores rebuked her calmly. "Her parents – my precious grandparents – reported it. My mom had stopped by the market on her way home from school that day and ran into you. She told her parents that you kept yelling and making fun of her – asking if she was going to pick up some poke salad. Luther was working at the market after dropping out of college. A few short weeks later, he'd leave for Vietnam."

"I don't know anything about that," Ming pleaded to the congregation of mourners.

"My mom told the police that Luther came to her rescue. He said he'd take his break if she'd like to go for a ride. Once they were in the car, his demeanor changed, and she became frightened," Delores shared. "He then pulled the car over, said something like, if you're Poke Salad Annie, then I'm the Gator that's going to get you. Chomp. Chomp. Then, he raped her. It's my understanding from that day on he wanted to be known as Gator."

Delores paused for everything to sink in. Diana and I looked at each other.

"But," she continued, "because of the scandal, it was kept a secret. When my mother became pregnant, she was sent away. The plan was for her to have the baby and then put it up for adoption. However, my mother died giving birth to me, and my grandparents couldn't go through with it. They ended up raising me."

Realizing she had lost control of the narrative, Ming got more agitated, turning to Gator's friend and loudly asking him if he believed what was being said. But he was too busy listening to Delores to answer her.

"I learned about my biological father several years ago and tried to contact Luther,"

Delores explained looking at the crowd. "The only number

I found was for Ming's business. When I told her why I wanted to speak with him, she made sure Gator never had anything to do with me. She threatened my grandparents by saying she would expose their 'tramp of a dead daughter to everyone in town.' Sound familiar? Didn't she just say something similar about this poor woman's daughter?"

"What do you want?" Ming yelled. "Why are you trying to ruin my husband's good name?"

"Your husband is responsible for ruining whatever name he had, and my mother's and the young woman you humiliated here today." Delores, still standing in the aisle, turned to face Ming. "Of course, Dottie Mae, *you* never had a good name, which is probably why you chose another – from where, some Chinese take-out menu? Your cover-up of Luther's sins is on you."

Delores turned and with her head held high, walked proudly out of the chapel. One by one, others began to leave. Gayle said she'd drive home with Connie. The rest of us, practically speechless, gathered in the parking lot.

"There are more girls," Diana said matter-of-factly. "While I was here, I spent some time going through old police reports."

"Why wasn't he arrested?" Maggie asked.

"No one ever went through with pressing charges," Diana explained. "They were too embarrassed, too ashamed. The detectives spoke with Gator a couple of times. He denied it, and no one was willing to take him to court."

"But Ming knew," Bobby said. "She had to have known."

"Maybe not," Diana replied. "Sure, one or two possibly. But she might not have known the extent of his actions. And, even then, she was in denial."

"Don't make her out to be a victim," Mike said strongly.

"No one is saying that," Peggy remarked. "She's every bit as bad as he was. All Diana was saying is that Ming might not have known everything. After all, she was his second wife. But you have to wonder how much the first wife knew, and if that's why their marriage crumbled."

"There might be something to that," Val added.

"Do you remember Dottie Mae or Ann from your school?" I asked Karen.

"No," Karen replied. "If they didn't go to my school or Mike's school, then they must have graduated from Central."

"Ming did," Mike added. "I mean Dottie Mae. I remember asking her when I realized we were the same age."

"Listen, tonight is our last night open until after the renovations," Maggie said. "If anyone wants to stop by and raise a glass, please do."

The rest of the afternoon had a somber feel to it. Mike was drained from the ordeal that Ming had put him through. But he realized it had been much worse for Connie, her daughter, and our new hero, Delores Payne. And yet, he wasn't willing to give Connie a pass for her actions over the past month.

"Do you think Connie knew who Ming was when I had them do her draperies?" Mike asked. "When Gator was in her home installing them?"

"No, because Connie didn't know Sara had been assaulted back then," I replied.

"But did Gator know whose home he was in?" Mike questioned.

"That I can't answer," I admitted. "Sara was married and not living there, so maybe not. Unless Connie had photographs of Sara displayed, and Gator put it together."

"Maybe one day we'll know Connie and Sara's side of the story," Mike mused.

Bobby called and said he and Karen would be there tonight, but he didn't know about Gayle. I was grateful he didn't include Connie's name in the mix. Dylan said they'd be back to Mike's home by six.

I put out leftovers from our lunch earlier in the day. After a snack, everyone started getting ready to go. Mike told us to go on without him. Nothing I could say would change his mind.

"What did Peggy say earlier?" Dylan asked Mike. "She said not to leave a man behind. We're not leaving you. If you want to stay home, then I guess we all will."

"Don't be silly," Mike said.

"I'm not," Dylan replied. "Trevor, will you let Peggy know we're not coming? Diana, can you text Karen and Bobby? I'll give Val a call."

"What the hell are you doing?" Mike said angrily.

"We're supporting our friend," Dylan replied. "Of course, that means we can't support our other friends Peggy and Maggie on this special night."

"You are such an asshole," Mike growled. "Point taken. Let me brush my teeth and run a comb through my hair, and then we can go. And wipe that silly grin off your face."

Charlie's was packed just like the old days. Peggy had saved us two booths since there wasn't space to stick a table out into the room with all the well-wishers.

"Now I see what Charlie's can become," Dylan said.

"Become again," Peggy corrected him. "This is how it was for years. The only spot in town for those of like minds to gather. Sugar started it back in the 1960s, and Charlie made sure it survived."

"True," I acknowledged, "But you're the one who kept it alive and are continuing to do so."

Suddenly, Mike became animated, stood on the bench seat, and yelled to get everyone's attention.

"Raise your glass in a toast to Sugar," he said.

"To Sugar," the crowd yelled and took a drink.

"Now, raise your glass in a toast to Charlie," he continued.

And the crowd followed suit.

"And finally, raise your glasses high to salute the one and only Peggy!" he exclaimed.

The crowd toasted then cheered the one who was the heart

of Charlie's – Peggy.

EPILOGUE

The next few weeks were an absolute madhouse as the renovation began. An existing wall came down, and a new wall was built to expand the kitchen. A new sink, work counter, ovens, refrigerator, freezer and stove were added or replaced. We installed dishwashing equipment and a pantry area with shelves for storage. It felt like one of the flip shows on TV where everyone works their magic, and at the end of the hour, they show off the results.

Painters were hard at work, and electricians added drop lights over the bar. Sconces floated on a wall of vintage-looking mirror tile installed behind the piano's future spot. The bathrooms were spiffed up with a fresh coat of paint and new fixtures. The booths were separated and lined end-to-end down the left wall. There was one booth section that didn't fit, so we decided to place it near the front door for anyone waiting for their reserved table.

We had not considered artwork for the wall above the banquette. However, a local artist had left his card with one of the workers when he heard it was going to become a piano bar. His work was colorful, whimsical, and music-themed – often with a piano keyboard motif. Mike and I met with him and discussed hanging his artwork with tags that showed it was for sale. He was happy for the exposure, and we were thrilled with the addition of non-budgeted original artwork.

When everything was in its place and professionally cleaned, we had the piano delivered on Thursday before the reopening on Saturday. Victor had made the arrangements. He had also scheduled a professional piano tuner to come on Friday to tweak it to perfection.

Dylan's menu, while limited, offered mouth-watering items designed to be shared. A sign on a wrought iron easel announced plans for a dinner menu and Sunday brunch coming soon.

The final inspection for the kitchen was the only thing we were waiting on. Mike had called a week earlier and was told they'd get to it as soon as possible. He reminded them that we had planned our grand reopening for Saturday and needed to be able to use the kitchen. They were not encouraging – short staffed and running behind. Peggy was beside herself. We *had* to open, and we *had* to have food. She vented her frustration to Karen when she called to check on things. Karen, in turn, mentioned it to Bobby.

Friday morning, an inspector appeared, surprising all of us. He checked and signed off on everything. We would be able to make our deadline.

"I'm so glad to see you," Peggy said to the beefy and bearded young man. "We got the impression that you guys were slammed and that we would have to reschedule our opening."

"You can thank Bobby for that," he replied. "He called me, and seriously, who can say no to Bobby?"

"How do you know him?" Mike asked.

"From Big Daddy's," he replied nonchalantly.

"The leather bar?" Maggie asked. "That's quite a coincidence. He was in there once – and he met you?"

"Once," our inspector-savior repeated with a sparkling

smile. "You must be mistaken. He's a regular. Everybody knows Bobby."

Somehow we managed to contain our laughter until he had left. Then all hell broke loose. Our Bobby – a leather daddy? However, we were so thankful that he was. Bobby had saved our asses.

Roberta Ann and Diana got to town Saturday morning, came straight to the house, and put their bags away in the two guest rooms.

Dylan and Trevor's rent to purchase proposal had been accepted. They immediately bought a bed, two chairs, a table, a lamp and moved in. After the grand opening, they'd sort through their things in Hillmont and decide what to move. Dylan had asked for a couple of things of Jim's if Diana didn't want them. She, in turn, asked for Jeff's dining table and chairs where we had shared "family" dinners.

The four of us had dressed in our finest and arrived at Charlie's Saturday evening at seven. Peggy had hired valet parkers for the special night. Diana and RA were blown away by the transformation of the bar. I have to say, Mike and

I were proud at how it had turned out. With the lights dimmed, it had the feeling of an intimate speakeasy from the past. A few other patrons had arrived and were either standing at the bar or seated at a table while the jukebox played.

Trevor looked handsome in a black shirt and pants, and Peggy and Maggie were quite fetching in their finery.

Three tables had been butted up against each other and draped in white tablecloths. A small sign illuminated by a flickering votive said: "Reserved for Family."

Val and Char, next to arrive, were all smiles taking in the room.

"Wow!" Val exclaimed. "I believe you boys know what you're doing. Have you ever considered a career in design?"

"Been there," Mike said.

"Done that," I added.

"Seriously, I'm impressed," Char commented.

I looked toward the front door and saw Karen and Gayle arrive, with Bobby following behind. They, too, went on and on about the new look.

"I thought you had a problem with the inspection," Karen said to Peggy.

"We did," Peggy admitted. "Fortunately, Bobby knew someone and called in a favor."

Realizing we now knew his secret, Bobby owned it by saying, "You just never know who you might meet in the strangest of places."

"I'm glad to see you, Gayle," Peggy said sincerely. "How is Connie? And, more importantly, how is her daughter?"

"It was embarrassing and something that Sara was forced to discuss with her husband," Gayle revealed. "Sadly, Connie is still not 'all back,' if you know what I mean. It's like she has Stockholm syndrome."

"Shall we take our seats?" Mike asked, changing the subject.

We ordered drinks and one each of everything on the menu. As we sat there visiting, more and more people arrived. Every table was now filled, along with every barstool. A crowd was forming in the open area toward the back. At seven-thirty, Victor sat down on the piano bench, introduced himself, and began to play something classical. He really was quite good. He then played some familiar show tunes and encouraged everyone to singalong. It was fun, festive, and exciting to once again see a crowd gathered at Charlie's having a good time.

The thought crossed my mind that no one was wearing a mask because we were eating and drinking. I said a quick prayer that nothing would put a damper on the grand reopening of Charlie's.

At eight-fifteen, Victor announced that he was going to take a short break. He encouraged us to drink up and promised to be back soon. Then Peggy marched to the front and banged on the piano to get everyone's attention.

"Normally, when Victor takes a break, we'd fire up the jukebox and encourage you to dance," she began. "However, on this special night, we have something else in mind."

"I wonder where this is going," Mike asked.

"I have a little story to tell you that happened during the renovation," she continued. "First of all, how about a round of applause for my dear friends Mike and Ricky, who are responsible for the beautiful makeover of Charlie's. That is, Charlie's Encore."

Peggy told us to stand, and no one ever says no to Peggy. We stood, and everyone applauded. It felt so good to be a part of the celebration. It also felt like I was where I was supposed to be at this time in my life.

"Everything was completed, and we had passed the inspection with flying colors," Peggy continued. "This gorgeous piano was delivered and yesterday morning Victor sent a piano tuner out to make sure it was ready for tonight. Well, let me just tell you that the repetitive bang, bang, bang from the tuning was getting on my last nerve. I told Maggie, Dylan and Trevor that I couldn't take it anymore and that I was going to lunch. I invited them to join me."

"Do you know what she's talking about?" I asked Mike, and he shook his head.

"Maggie and Dylan said yes, but Trevor volunteered to stay behind until the tuner guy had finished," Peggy added. "We promised to bring something back for him and then slipped out the back door."

She motioned for Trevor to join her.

"I was the first one through the door when we returned and immediately felt chills run through my body. Someone was playing the piano and singing the most soulful version of Dolly Parton's 'Jolene' I had ever heard. You know, Dolly wrote that song about a beautiful redheaded vixen – just like me in my youth," Peggy, said laughing.

One of the bartenders yelled out: "You still are, mama!"

"Anyway, I put my hand up to shush Dylan and Maggie, and we stood in the kitchen and listened," she admitted. "I assumed it had to be the piano tuner but, Dylan knew differently. It was Trevor. This beautiful young man, who you better be tipping big time tonight, was bringing me to tears."

"Did you know?" I asked Diana and RA, who were as surprised as me.

"Now, he's a bit nervous," Peggy announced. "I asked him to share his talent with you during this brief break. Trevor?"

Trevor gave us a nervous smile, sat down on the piano bench, and started to play. After a long piano introduction – that was probably his way of calming his nerves – he began to sing a slow and emotional version of Dolly's signature song. Like Peggy, I felt chills. Dylan stepped out from the kitchen and stood off to one side with the biggest smile I had ever seen. When Trevor finished, everyone who wasn't already standing stood as the room erupted with applause. I almost felt sorry for Victor having to follow him. But he took it in stride, hugged Trevor, and continued with his act.

"What do you think?" Peggy asked when she returned to our table.

"I'm blown away. I heard that he could sing, but I never knew he could play," I said.

"By ear, no less," Peggy explained. "He said he had a couple of years of lessons when he was a kid. And he sang in the school choir. It's a natural gift. Even Dylan didn't know he could play. Trevor's never had a piano of his own."

"He does now," Diana announced. "Tell Victor we're coming to see him Monday, and the James Norris Foundation will be buying Trevor a piano."

I looked toward the group of revelers standing in the back and spotted Connie. I nodded to Gayle, who got up and walked toward her. Mike noticed them together and his body became rigid. A few minutes later, Gayle returned to the table and Connie was gone.

"What happened?" Mike asked as the others who had missed the exchange turned toward us.

"I told her this is not the time or place. This is Peggy's night, along with Dylan, Maggie and Trevor. I also told her that when the time *was* right, she owed you an apology and an explanation. Regardless of what she was going through, she turned her back on all of us. We are family, and yet she didn't trust us enough to ask for our help," Gayle shared.

Just then, Trevor came over to check on our drinks. Everyone engulfed him with kisses and hugs. I couldn't help but think back to that Valentine's Day when Jim insisted that we all go to Tattinger's and meet Trevor. Jim knew before any of us that he needed to be part of our family.

"Gayle," Mike whispered, taking her hand as she turned to face him. "Thank you."